Vangelis Hatziyannidis was born in 1967 in Serres and lives in Athens. He studied law at Athens University and drama at the Veakis school. He worked as an actor for three years before taking up writing. His first novel, *Four Walls* won Greek literary magazine *Diavazo*'s prize for the best new writer in 2001 and has been translated into French, Italian and Spanish. The French edition of *Four Walls* won the Laure Bataillon Prize for the best foreign book and best translation of the year.

Anne-Marie Stanton-Ife studied Modern and Mediaeval Languages at Cambridge University and Comparative Literature at University of London. Since leaving univeristy she has spent time teaching in both the UK and Greece, as well as working as a translator. She currently lives in Athens.

four walls

Published in Great Britain and the United States in 2006 by
MARION BOYARS PUBLISHERS LTD
24 Lacy Road, London SW15 1NL
www.marionboyars.co.uk

Distributed in Australia and New Zealand by
Peribo Pty Ltd, 58 Beaumont Road, Kuring-gai, NSW 2080

First published in Greece by To Rodakio as *Oi Tesseris Toichoi* in 2000

Printed in 2006
10 9 8 7 6 5 4 3 2 1

A CIP catalogue record for this book is available from the British Library.
A CIP catalog record for this book is available from the Library of Congress.

With thanks to the European Commission Euclid Culture 2000 for assistance
with the translation of this book.

ISBN 0-7145-3122-7
13 digit ISBN 9780-7145-3122-9

Set in Bembo 11/14pt
Printed in England by Bookmarque Ltd

four walls

by

Vangelis Hatziyannidis

Translated by Anne-Marie Stanton-Ife

MARION BOYARS

LONDON • NEW YORK

the experiment

That Rodakis was not an irascible man was a matter of record. There were occasions in his life when anybody else would have exploded, justifiably giving vent to their pent-up rage, while he would merely curl his upper lip in an expression of displeasure, and even then only fleetingly, like the time when his sister borrowed his book on botany. That old volume, bound inside a soft leather slipcase with the outline of an apple tree tooled on the cover, was very dear to him. It had been published in the previous century and contained an index of plants, covering all the trees and flowers of the Mediterranean. He had acquired it in Italy at a time when he was virtually penniless. She had borrowed it on some absurd pretext, promising to return it within a week. Two weeks later, he had to ask for it back. As soon as she saw him, she burst into tears. In between sobs, the words, 'I'm so useless; so useless,' broke through, again and again.

His sister had regularly demonstrated the truth of this proposition, so this was not news to him. What he could not understand was why she felt the need to tell him this now. The buzzing in his right ear started up almost instantly, the same buzzing he experienced whenever fear penetrated his soul. And it was fear in all its magnificence that was overtaking him at that moment; fear accompanied by the suspicion that the phrase 'I'm so useless' might, however remotely, be connected with his book. It was. The book was ruined. Stained, then eaten.

'The kitchen gets the sun in the morning – lovely morning sun. I was sitting over there leafing through the book, admiring the beautiful illustrations, the delicate little flowers, the leaves, the roots while I boiled up the strawberries for the jam you like so much – I was making it for you really; I don't much like strawberry, as you know. Well – just as I was taking the saucepan off the heat to put it down on the marble worktop – I've no idea how it happened, but it slipped onto my arm, right here, and without thinking I let go of it, I mean I dropped it. It hit the marble, and the whole thing capsized; the hot jam went oozing all over your book there where I'd left it, open on the worktop. I nearly died. My limbs went numb, buckled under me and I collapsed onto the floor. I don't know how long for; two, five, maybe ten minutes. When I came to and opened my eyes, what did I see but the dog, up on its hind legs, its front paws on the worktop, slurping up the jam? I screeched "Leo!" and as soon as he heard me, he clamped the book tight between his teeth and made off with it. There was nothing left of it – except some chewed up bits of leather I found in his corner.'

As her narrative drew to a close, the tears started again. Rodakis's only reaction was to curl his upper lip. But that was not the mad part about it.

Much later, through an unbelievable series of coincidences, he discovered that his book had never been destroyed at all, and that his sister's absurd tale about the accident with the jam and her dog devouring the book was nothing more than a perverse fabrication, invented with the sole purpose of gaining possession of something which did not belong to her. When he found out, he simply curled his upper lip. Now that *was* mad.

However, there was one thing that could make him lose his self-possession: people interfering with his things. In fact, he considered the destruction of his property to be a less serious misdemeanour than disturbing their position. This was a point the few people who ever lived with him were very clear about, so the chances of Rodakis ever losing his composure were kept to a minimum.

One of those rare occasions took place that very afternoon, all on account of a silver teaspoon. For as long as anyone could remember, the silver teaspoon had been kept in the pocket of a green silk dressing gown. The dressing gown itself had long since outlived its purpose but one of the pockets had been preserved out of a sentimental attachment to the once exquisite fabric. Wrapped inside it was the silver spoon Rodakis had been given by his father, S. Rodakis.

That afternoon, when the moment he had been waiting for finally came, he opened the drawer the silver was kept in; had he not been in possession of such a remarkable nervous system, he would have been trembling with anticipation. He dug deeper in the drawer, under the pile of tea towels, and saw that the spoon in the silk pocket was missing. His daughter Rosa, about thirteen years old at the time, was sitting at the kitchen table trying to finish off a plate of peas. She immediately sensed that something was terribly wrong, even though she couldn't pinpoint it. She identified a peculiar glint in her father's eye and it seemed as though all the metal blades of the knives lying in the drawer were reflected in a threatening, grey light in his face.

A second later the drawer, violently wrested from the dresser, upended itself in mid-air, flooding the tiled floor with its contents: soupspoons, teaspoons, large and small forks.

'Where's grandpa's silver spoon?'

'I don't know – could it have fallen down the back into the drawer underneath by mistake?' suggested Rosa, breathlessly.

The drawer below was inverted in turn and all its serving spoons and forks, tongs and spatulas ended up on the floor. Somewhere, in the midst of this metal heap, there was a faint green glimmer. He unwrapped the silver spoon, removed it from the fabric and shook it menacingly in front of Rosa's face, which by now had turned almost white. Then he left.

The episode would have taken on even greater proportions had he not been so anxious to get down to the cellar. Guided only by the light coming in from the two fanlights, he moved among all the bulky objects that had been stored down there for years and stopped in front of some shelves. On the middle one stood three clay storage-jars. He took one of them down and opened it. He plunged the silver spoon deep inside, and pulled it out, the bowl now full. He twirled it round between his fingers two or three times before putting it in his mouth.

A tiny cherub fluttered across the ceiling, drifting from corner to corner while the brass notes of lovingly-polished trumpets sounded in the distance as the vivid aroma escaped through the gaps under the door, until it had permeated the entire house.

S. Rodakis, long since dead, had been a bee-keeper with enough hives to keep at least half the island in honey. There was a time when he had so many orders that he couldn't keep up with them. For ten years in a row, he was literally overwhelmed with work, and he no longer sold unlabelled honey wholesale. He developed his own packaging in metal tins and pasted specially-printed labels bearing his name with the picture of a bee under it and under the bee the legend:

PURE HONEY
FROM UNTRODDEN FORESTS

The 'untrodden' part was not strictly true. Entire flocks of sheep grazed in those forests, day-trippers visited them during the summer months and lovers chased each other round them. Not that anyone or anything ever distracted the bees from their labours – and it is doubtful whether the honey would have tasted any better had the forest been genuinely 'untrodden'. Nevertheless, the word 'untrodden' had played no small part in the commercial success of the Rodakis honey. It would not be too much of an exaggeration to claim that he owed his large stone house as well as the land that he bought on the island during this period to the appeal of the 'untrodden', because the quality of the honey, although undoubtedly superior, did not in itself justify the excessive demand for it.

In the tenth year, everything changed. It was the year of the great fire that ravaged the entire northern section of the island; not a single bee, hive or forest, untrodden or otherwise, escaped. The house, built in a clearing in the forest with low-lying vegetation all around, survived. S. Rodakis was devastated; he knew he was finished unless he started from scratch somewhere else. But he quickly set out on another train of thought: packing up and seeking out another 'untrodden' forest was out of the question. He was too old even to consider it. His hives had given him a great deal. Thanks to them, he had purchased land and turned it over to cultivation, which brought him a substantial annual income. One option was of course to sit quietly at home and enjoy the fruits of his labours until his dying day. Perhaps he should be grateful for this turn of events. As for his children, they gave him no real cause for concern, either of them. The daughter had married and left home, which was a source of immeasurable relief. The son, for his part seemed, more or less, to have grown out of all that nonsense about seeing things that used to trouble him as a child. Although he had originally intended to put him in the honey business, after the fire and the inevitable changes it brought, he abandoned the idea. Rodakis had suddenly seemed to take an interest in farming, which his father encouraged, reasoning that his fields would increase their yield as a result. He spent hours in the fields talking to the farmers about everything from the special features of each plant to propagation techniques and plant diseases; in only two years he had become as much of an expert as any university-educated agronomist.

One February evening, Rodakis was sitting in what was known

as the big room (which served as a makeshift sitting-room) listing the tasks that needed to be carried out the following day. Suddenly, S. Rodakis walked in, holding an empty basket with an urgent look on his face, the look of a man who is unforgivably late. His son was momentarily surprised because he had thought the old man had been asleep for hours.

'I'm off to do the grapes,' he said.

'What grapes?'

'If they're left there much longer, the turtledoves will get at them.'

That was that. His mind had set off on a journey to an unknown destination, and there was no turning back. He could sustain the occasional logical conversation, but as time wore on, these brief interludes of lucidity became increasingly rare. He would frequently disappear, only to be found hours later up a tree, or inside a wardrobe. Later on he started to develop peculiar habits: he would pull up all the floorboards, tie the curtains into large knots, tirelessly dig enormous holes in the garden, fill them up with all the clothes he could get his hands on. And sit on them.

One day, inspecting the heavy wool overcoat he was wearing, he decided that it was threadbare and needed to be disposed of, so he went outside and set fire to it. Without taking it off first.

Seven years had passed since the fire ravaged the 'untrodden' forest.

After S. Rodakis's death and the erroneous assumption that he had committed suicide (which prompted extensive soul-searching on the part of the priest before he could be persuaded to perform proper burial rites), his beneficiaries, Rodakis and his sister, had to decide how to divide the inheritance. The daughter made it clear that after her father's horrific death, she could never bring herself to live in that house again, and wanted absolutely nothing to do with it. (The truth was that she had calculated that since she already owned a house, it would make more sense for her to secure a regular income from the fields, rather than end up with an empty, useless old building.)

So Rodakis was left with the house and the two fields that were his due – one five, the other ten thousand square metres. He sold off the larger plot almost immediately in order to finance an old dream of his: a journey to the ends of the earth.

He was away for seven months, taking in Egypt, China, India and a tour of the major European cities on the return leg. His last stop was ancient Pompeii, and from there he travelled to Naples, where he picked up an old volume in a leather slip-case called *Botany* in one of the city's antiquarian bookshops, leaving him with just enough money to pay for his passage home.

He made a point of buying something from all the places he visited. When he got home, he gathered together all these objects and put them in a cupboard, spending hours deciding how best to arrange them. Now and then he would open what he called his 'cupboard of valuables' and take a look at his treasures. On rare occasions, he would invite somebody else to share the sight with him.

Something significant happened to him on his travels. He was in Egypt, staying at the poetically named Moonlight Pyramid Hotel. After his visit to the pyramids, he was so overwhelmed by the sight of the majestic monuments that even hours later, he was quite unable to fall asleep. Until that point he had hardly given any thought to the island and the recent unpleasantness. That night, an image from the past suddenly came to him. He could not define with any certainty when it had happened, beyond the fact that it was from the time after his father's descent into dementia: S. Rodakis was standing in front of a window, looking out.

As soon as father saw son coming, he beckoned to him, saying it was time to take him into his confidence, and to share the details of a secret plan he had been working on for some time. At first Rodakis tried to avoid the conversation, and attempted to send his father off to bed, but the old man got angry and he was forced to listen. At the time he did not attach any importance to his father's words, and simply waited for the outburst to finish so he could get back to work. Nothing about the episode struck him as out of the ordinary at the time.

The fact that he was in range of the pyramids' field of energy may have sparked off the recurrence of this scene in his memory. Why were his father's incoherent words, the product of a disturbed mind, appearing to him like an epiphany? What was the significance of them?

He found some of the hotel's headed notepaper in the drawer of his bedside table and jotted down some of the old man's phrases; he was worried that after the recent bombardment of new impressions and images his brain had been receiving on a daily basis (and would continue to do so for some time), he would be unable to recall the details.

The Moonlight Pyramid was bathed in silence.

When he got back on the island, he knew he had some important decisions to make. He had been of age for some time. He was twenty-five years old and essentially unemployed. His dabbling with the family land had come to an end when the fields passed into his sister's ownership. Career opportunities on the island were limited to a choice of farmer, builder, priest – or cobbler – cobblers were always in demand. After some thought, he decided to go and work as an apprentice to a builder who spent most of his time working on the southern side of the island. Rodakis was a fast learner and instinctively knew that he would like the work. Why a man of his background would choose to go into building instead of farming was anybody's guess. Perhaps it was because he suspected that farming was not where his true talents lay.

One Sunday afternoon, he spotted the figures of the parish

priest and the president of the village council making their way up the hill to his house.

They said they had come on very important business and needed to talk to him. The priest spoke first.

'You know, when we do good to others we are really helping ourselves. In fact, we should be grateful to them for giving us a chance to save our souls. But you already know that. We're here to offer just such an opportunity, and you'd do well to take advantage of it.'

'Take as much time as you need to think it over,' interjected the president, 'nobody is putting any pressure on you – but please bear in mind that the matter is of some urgency, and too much procrastination never got anybody anywhere.'

'What is it? Tell me,' said Rodakis, who was sure he could feel his right ear buzzing.

'Don't worry,' said the priest. Having sat through countless confessions, he could pick up on even the subtlest of fluctuations in the conscience of his interlocutors. 'We have come here to discuss something quite...' He hesitated, and for want of a better word, had to settle for 'simple'. 'Go on,' he said, urging the president to take over.

'The day before yesterday, a woman arrived on the island. My wife found her down at the harbour sitting on a trunk, sobbing. She'd been on her way somewhere else, but they put her off the boat here – she hadn't got a ticket, you see.'

'She's in a terrible state,' added the priest. 'Like she regularly takes a good beating.'

'We asked her what the matter was, but she got everything mixed up, and with her sobbing and sniffing it was impossible to get any sense out of her. Who knows if there is any truth to her story, anyway?'

'She's got a limp too – God bless her. Poor, miserable creature; you've got to feel sorry for her.'

'What do you want me to do, Father?' asked Rodakis who,

after listening to the priest *humming*-and-*ha-ing* about good deeds, was in no doubt that all this was being laid on for his benefit.

'Listen. The state she's in, no family would ever take her in, even if they had the room. Nobody. Anyway – who has got that kind of space? Nobody except you, that is. You've got an entire house to yourself, three floors, counting the basement. Stick her in one of the rooms down there for a while, just 'til she gets back on her feet, and we'll take it from there. We can't have her roaming the countryside – she'll be eaten by jackals.'

'Where is she now?' asked Rodakis.

'I let her spend a couple of nights in the church, behind the candle stand. I can't have her sleeping in my house, in with the orphans; who knows what might get into her in the middle of the night?'

'Oh, wonderful,' thought Rodakis. 'The man's too nervous to have her in his own house at night, so now he's trying to offload her onto me.'

He plucked up the courage to ask, 'What might "get into her" in the middle of the night – what do you mean?'

'Nothing will "get into her,"' said the president. 'You'll see, once she's feeling better, she'll start making herself useful round the house. I'm not suggesting you take her on as your housemaid; that's not what we're talking about here, but she will be an extra pair of hands. It's only temporary. Until she's on her feet again.'

'Anyway, looks like she's got a good few years on you,' added the priest.

'People won't get the wrong idea, that's what the priest means.'

'If I catch anyone spreading rumours, I'll send them straight to hell without any rites,' said the priest with menace in his voice. 'Listen, it's not that I want to put any pressure on you, but I'll be extremely disappointed if you say no.'

Rodakis agreed to take in the woman on a temporary basis; he would have agreed even without all the speeches. It would have been enough for him to be told that somebody needed a room. He would not have objected at all; his house was certainly big enough, and giving somebody the use of a room did not cost him anything. As long as they didn't interfere with his things. Yes. That had to be made clear. That was a basic condition.

A few hours later one of the priest's orphans brought the woman up to Rodakis's house, left her at the fence and disappeared. Her name was Vaya. She wore stiff black clothes full of white stains, like dried out tidemarks, and her body gave off an odour reminiscent of putrefied seaweed.

The first few minutes of their acquaintance were buoyed along by her sobs, and then silence when she realized that the man standing before her was not in the least moved by her performance; nor did it look like he was going to bombard her with questions like everybody else did, so there was no need to shield herself behind her tears. If anything, he seemed almost indifferent to her. He said that the priest would be making arrangements for her, but in the meantime, he didn't mind if she stayed. He gave her his father's old bedroom, the only downstairs bedroom. As soon as she was confident that she had secured shelter and a space of her own, she spoke.

'I won't be any trouble. As long as I can keep to the house and the garden.'

He explained that he was out of the house most of the day, and because he didn't work locally, he left very early in the morning and came back late in the evening. He gave her the freedom of the kitchen, and told her to take all the fruit and vegetables she wanted from the garden, making it very clear that he only ever had his evening meal at home. Finally, he broached the delicate subject:

'The only thing I will ask of you,' he said, 'is not to touch my things. When I need something, I expect to find it in its proper place.'

Vaya looked him in the eye for the first time.

'I'm not a thief.'

'That's not what I meant. I meant that you mustn't touch my things – that's what I meant. I don't want my things interfered with.'

She shook her head as if giving a pledge, at which a black insect emerged from the edge of one her eyebrows, and after traversing her temple, disappeared into the pitch darkness of her hair. Sensing something, she immediately brought her finger up for a scratch, but it was too late. The insect had already made its way to safety.

'I've got a couple of trunks,' she said.

'Where are they?'

'The priest's boy is bringing them up this evening.'

'Big?'

'Big.'

'They won't fit in the bedroom then. We'll put them in the back storeroom. It's almost empty. I don't use it. We'll keep them there.'

Vaya's arrival made no difference to Rodakis's routine; everything went on as normal for the simple reason that he never saw her. The minute he walked through the door in the evenings, she would lock herself away in her room and never re-emerge. The first week passed without a word and without his laying eyes on her once. He did not know what to make of it. If it hadn't been for the occasional muffled sound coming from the direction of her bedroom, he might have thought she had left. The house, in keeping with the ground rules he had been so anxious to establish, seemed completely untouched. In the garden, however, he did notice that a row of cabbages had been planted in the neglected rudimentary melon field on the edge of his property. He also discovered that the priest had arranged for one of the villagers to bring milk up to the house for her every morning. There were no other signs of life. He wondered whether the abrupt manner in which he had spoken to her on her arrival had put her off, or worse, scared her. On the other hand, he was relieved that he wasn't expected to sit and talk to a poor unfortunate woman every evening when he came home exhausted from work. Even so, her total non-appearance made him strangely uneasy. It felt like he was living with a ghost who never showed itself but whose presence could nonetheless be felt.

His father's old bedroom had one serious disadvantage: it had no independent access to the rest of the house. Its only door opened onto the big room, which you had to cross to get in and get out. Rodakis used to spend a lot of time in the big room before turning in for the night. But ever since the woman had been installed in the inner room, he had been reluctant to sit there and would do so just long enough to take a quick look at his belongings, and then he would go straight to bed.

One night, when she'd already been there for ten days, he thought he should perhaps knock on her door, ask if all was well and see if she needed anything. It was only polite. He hesitated, worrying that he might be disturbing her. She might be asleep and he didn't want to wake her; or worse, frighten her. He stood there for some time, staring in indecision at the door.

He had almost convinced himself to leave things be and to restrict himself to what he had done so far − providing accommodation, nothing else − when his gaze fell on the keyhole, and the temptation to steal a glimpse insinuated itself into his conscience.

He knew that as soon as the temptation took root, the damage had been done; sooner or later he would have to give in, so he decided to get it over with quickly and not waste time on a pointless dilemma. He stood up and walked across to her door, and without any further deliberation, pushed his eye up against the tiny hole.

A quantity of air suddenly escaped from his heart, and shot up into his vocal chords with such force that if he hadn't managed to send it back down at the last minute, it would have exploded into a deafening scream that would have audible as far away as the forest. His eye had encountered another eye, a frozen, colourless eye conducting its own investigations from the other side of the door.

'She's spying on me.' The thought filled him with panic; nevertheless, he managed to marshal what little self-possession he had left to move away from the door. A strange, mysterious creature was living under his roof, spying on him. Fear pervaded his soul as he recalled the words of the priest: 'I can't have her sleeping in my house, in with the orphans'. He locked his bedroom door and draped a shirt over the door handle to block the keyhole. But he couldn't sleep.

After that night, everything changed. The minute he got home from work, he would go straight upstairs, lock his bedroom door and only emerge in the morning when he would rush out to work. He never went into the big room anymore, and she remained unseen and invisible behind her own locked door. Rodakis felt her presence all around him, everywhere, which he found increasingly unsettling. He wanted to be free of her, to get her out of his house, but he didn't have the nerve to do that either. He just sat passively in his closed room, impotent and petrified.

The stress of the situation had consequences. His old delusional symptoms resurfaced. He started hearing noises and seeing things, something that added to his distress and kept him awake at night. All this in combination with a physically demanding job brought him to the verge of collapse, which only compounded his feelings of vulnerability and helplessness in the face of a nightmare he had willingly invited into his home.

One day, while carrying out repairs to a roof, he passed out and fell off the building. Fortunately, the ground beneath him had just been dug up. He was quickly carried home and the doctor arrived shortly thereafter. Apart from the numerous sprains, scratches and bruises he had acquired, the doctor diagnosed extreme physical exhaustion.

'Have me admitted to the hospital,' he begged the doctor, who found him inexplicably anxious.

'I don't think that will be necessary.'

'You've got to get me to a hospital, doctor. I beg you.'

'Relax. Your condition is not that serious; nothing a few days of bed rest won't take care of. But you must calm down.'

'Please – I'd be better off in hospital…'

The doctor, unable to make sense of this insistence, decided to give him a shot to relax him. Rodakis was soon asleep. On his way out, the doctor bumped into the priest who had heard about the accident.

'How is he?'

'He was lucky. The fall was not too bad, considering where he fell from.'

'God bless him! How did he manage to fall anyway?'

'Fainted. He's exhausted. But with a little rest he should be back on his feet in no time. Probably some mild concussion there too. He's very confused – the fall must have given him quite a fright – kept asking to go to hospital. I gave him something; he's fast asleep now.'

As soon as the doctor left, the priest went upstairs, looked in on the invalid, then went back downstairs and knocked on Vaya's door.

As a boy, Rodakis used to enjoy his hallucinations. Were it not for the fact that he got a good thrashing every time he mentioned them, it would never have occurred to him that there was anything wrong with them. They were never frightening; they were just a game his mind played, a game he played alone and one that only he understood. He soon realized that if he wanted to keep out of trouble he had better keep quiet about them. One day, however, when a high temperature was keeping the windmills of his imagination turning, he was unable to restrain himself. During a meal he and his sister were having with their father, he stood up and announced: 'A horse is rolling on its back in the garden!' S. Rodakis got up and struck the boy with force across his right cheek. The blow found his ear too and hours later, it was still buzzing. That was the last time he said anything on the subject of his hallucinations. His ear was not permanently damaged, but after that, whenever he sensed trouble, that he might be in for a beating, the same buzzing sound would return, as though in advance warning. These symptoms never completely disappeared, and the buzzing recurred every time he was in the grip of fear. He was familiar with this pattern and would silently whisper, 'I hear fear'.

As he grew older, his hallucinations became less frequent and eventually stopped altogether. He had never regarded them as something to worry about, for him they were images, just harmless, innocent images, a thing of the past, part of his childhood. Until they came back, that is. And their return coincided with the arrival of the invisible stranger.

The effects of the tranquillizer wore off after four hours. His right ankle, right knee, left shoulder and ribcage all hurt horribly. He tried to sit up only to discover that his back was in even more pain. His first thought was that the doctor had refused to send him to hospital and he was all alone, injured and defenceless, trapped inside his house with the stranger. After an enormous effort, he managed to prop himself up on the edge of his bed. Shifting from a horizontal to a vertical position seemed to help restore his mind to a more logical plane: What did he have to fear from a poor unfortunate woman with nothing to her name? A woman who must be feeling, even if she had not said as much, hopelessly indebted to him for his generosity, for giving her a roof over her head without asking for the slightest thing in return.

A yellow butterfly fluttered drunkenly past his window. This raised his spirits even more; life was so simple, and there he was, trying to burden it with obsessive, groundless fears. All that seemed so ridiculous to him now that he couldn't suppress his laughter: the poor creature didn't dare so much as move as long as he was there, and not even the fact that she was spying on him through her keyhole could justify causing him such alarm. After all, wasn't that exactly what he was trying to do – look into her bedroom of all places? The yellow butterfly reappeared, its wings trembling. Some of the strength was returning to his limbs. He lay down again, allowing his body to sink deep into his bed and luxuriate in its soft embrace.

A small shot was heard. It came from downstairs. Silence. Then a few footsteps. Then nothing. More footsteps. Nothing. Someone was wandering around down there; not somebody. Vaya. But she never left her room when he was at home. So why today? Why now when he was on his back and unable to react?

The courage he had rediscovered was short-lived; it soon disappeared, mimicking the uncertain flight of the butterfly. Once again, he was in the throes of fear, which had entered through his ear. He tried to get up. His left ankle, wrapped in the makeshift splint the doctor had made, was unable to support his weight. He finally worked out that crawling along on all fours, despite the minor injuries to his knee, was the most efficient way to move about. He crawled out of his room and darted as quickly as he could into the next room, his sister's old bedroom. At least from there he could get a clear view of the stairs and see any threatening moves in good time to react. He lay face down on the floor in the darkness keeping watch through the half-open door. The sounds continued as before, but there was still no sign of her. Not at first. A short while later, he heard footsteps coming up the stairs, steadily and confidently. No hesitation. No guilt. No mercy.

As the footsteps reached the end of their course, Rodakis passed out.

For the third time that day, he experienced the strange sensation of waking up and not knowing where he was, why he was where he was, or how he had got there. The first time was when he came round after the accident and managed to make out the face of the doctor looking down at him; the second time was after the effects of the injection had worn off; the third time was when he opened his eyes after he had fainted and saw the bookcase of the big room standing across from him and Vaya's wide-open bedroom door right next to him. He was downstairs. He must have been carried there: Nothing made sense! He was no longer master of his house, no longer master of himself. Now, with him lying there, injured and paralyzed she – who he'd taken in out of the kindness of his heart – was showing her true colours. She had come out of hiding, aware that she had the upper hand now, and started moving freely around the house. The sounds that kept reaching him were proof of this. He was only sorry that he had not asked the doctor to help him, but resolved to fight his fear and confront her: he would ask her to leave. He would throw her out.

Vaya came into the room and looked at him with her big colourless eyes.

'You awake?' she asked. 'The priest told me to keep an eye on you.'

'How did I end up downstairs?' asked Rodakis.

'I carried you. You had fallen flat on your face, and I thought, if I put him on his bed, he might get up and try to go downstairs and fall again. That's why I brought you down, because I'm cooking and this way I won't have to worry about you.'

'How did you get me down all those stairs?'

'Lifted you. On my back.'

'Aren't I too heavy for you?'

Vaya laughed. This was the first time he'd seen her laugh. Her teeth were perfect – they looked like they'd never been used.

'Too heavy? You should try lifting my trunks!'

A short while into the conversation Rodakis made the following comparisons between this and his first impression of Vaya: her hair and her clothes had been washed and had shed their sheen of plaster dust; all signs of imminent sobbing were gone – on the contrary, there was something robust about her now, a somewhat feral strength. Finally, there was nothing to suggest that she was mentally defective in any way; the way she spoke gave the impression that she was probably quite sharp.

He told her that he wanted to go up to his room, thereby putting off asking her to leave. She made him promise not to try to get out of bed on his own, and, despite his protests, hauled him up onto her back, which made her stoop sufficiently for both his feet to clear the floor. She mounted the staircase without showing the slightest hint of strain or any sign of the difficulty the disability in her leg with the limp had to be causing her.

A little while later she brought him up a bowl containing a deep red steaming hot liquid. Rodakis could not place the smell.

'Beetroot soup,' she informed him. 'Never tried it?'

Not only had he never tired it, he had no idea that such a thing existed. It had a very strong taste, and judging by the sweet burning sensation it left in his throat, he concluded that there was both vinegar and honey in it. He was just about to tell her that he did not like it, that her bittersweet concoction was as close to disgusting as you could get, when he suddenly buckled to its charms and felt the lure of a second, definitely last, spoonful. Only it wasn't his last.

'More?' she asked after watching him drain his bowl.

'Just half.'

The fear had gone. All of a sudden, magically, he seemed to have shaken off not only the fear specific to Vaya, but a more generalized fear too. He was confident that never again would he be scared of anyone or anything; it was as if he had been inoculated against it.

'Why were you hiding?' he asked her after his third half bowl.

'I've learned not to tempt fate.'

This enigmatic answer hung in the air together with the smell of beetroot.

'Don't. You don't have to shut yourself away.'

Vaya nodded and picked up his bowl.

Ever since Rosa was little, the only sure way of getting her to do – or not do – something was to promise to tell her a secret. It didn't matter what kind of secret it was, or who or what it was about; all she needed to hear was 'I'll tell you a secret,' and she would do anything you asked of her.

Rodakis often exploited this weakness of hers, promising secrets when he didn't have the least idea what kind of secret he would have to produce when the time came for his daughter to collect. Most secrets were invented on the spur of the moment – and were not particularly inspired either. Were it not for the fact that they carried the label 'secret', they would have passed off as insignificant pieces of information. The mere idea that there were only a privileged few who knew, for example, that the president of the village council had a two-fingered cousin; or that the cobbler, long since deceased, used to hide his money in a hollow shoe-tree; or that a long time ago there was a woman on the island who used to catch cats and chop off their tails with an axe, made Rosa feel very rich, that she was in possession of information which under certain circumstances she might be able to trade for services – that is, if she found someone with a similar weakness. Until such a time, she was content to store these rare treasures in her head, where they could neither be heard nor read.

'If someone knows a secret nobody else does, and if that person dies, is the secret lost forever?'

It seemed an imponderable injustice to her that there should be secrets that go to waste. Her father tried to reassure her, saying that people generally confided their secrets, at least the important ones, before they died. She was not satisfied. What about the people who don't? That was when Rodakis came up with the idea of the ledgers.

When someone had a secret known only to them, and they took that secret to the grave, that secret was automatically entered in the great ledgers in outer space, which exist precisely to fulfil this function. One necessary condition for a secret to be recorded was that it was completely inaccessible to the world. For example, a secret, one that no living person knows, if it has been written down somewhere, in a letter for instance, or on the wall of some cave, or on a piece of paper hidden away in a box (now this was not a random example), it would not be recorded since all the possibilities of discovery had not been exhausted. Rosa imagined these massive ledgers, so heavy they were impossible to lift, lying wide open, suspended somewhere in the dark universe. They were more precious in her eyes than any buried treasure or any knowledge she could hope to gain – more precious even than the best encyclopedia. According to Rodakis (who found the business of firing Rosa's imagination extremely diverting) the ledgers were the unique records of the secret revelations of great scientists, which if made generally known, could change the lives of people on Earth in the course of a single day. Unfortunately, only the souls of the dead had access to them.

This last fact had an unexpected consequence on Rosa's childish spirit, one Rodakis never suspected. Every evening, before she went to sleep, she would beseech God in her prayers to allow her to die in her sleep to give her the chance to leaf through one of those giant ledgers. On waking, she would note with disappointment that her prayers had not been answered.

After the positive encouragement she was given, Vaya came out of hiding. On a number of evenings they sat at the table together, sharing the meals she prepared – most of which consisted of unusual combinations that were slightly peculiar but absolutely irresistible nonetheless. He never missed a chance to tell her that she must never interfere with his possessions, making the point that the increased familiarity between them did not release her from the conditions he had originally stipulated.

Around that time, there was a sudden surge in demand for builders. For some reason, everyone on the island wanted to build a new house or, failing that, restore their existing home. Word soon got round that Rodakis had developed into a master craftsman of considerable talent and industry, and there was a growing list of people asking him to oversee their building work. This meant he could leave his job as a builder's assistant and start looking for an assistant of his own.

A young man of about seventeen came to find him, desperate for work. He had to raise enough money to save his sister's vineyards from the clutches of loan sharks. Rodakis, feeling the way he did about his own sister, was amazed.

'Do you really love her so much?' he asked, trying to mask his curiosity.

'Only her,' replied the boy, without repeating the words 'I love.'

He explained that as soon as he had raised the money, he planned to enter the monastery. None of this made any sense to Rodakis, but the boy seemed pleasant enough so he took him on immediately. His name was Paschalis, and he was needed for increasingly long hours as the work kept piling up. Neither of them complained: one was urgently in need of money and the other considered it an honour that an ever-increasing proportion of the islanders was showing confidence in him.

As a result Rodakis was hardly ever home and Vaya was alone most of the time. Up to that point she had complied with the restrictions placed on her with almost religious zeal. She would move about the house with trepidation, terrified that without her realizing it, a piece of paper lying on his desk in the big room might get blown off by the force of the air gathering under her skirt as she walked past; or that some tool or one of the kitchen utensils would get moved. This anxiety was like a noose around her neck, and she was terrified that one false move would be enough for it to tighten and throttle her.

There were also times when she was overwhelmed by a desire to turn the entire house upside down: pull all the books down onto the floor; tip all the clothes out of the wardrobes and replace them with saucepans thrown in with hammers and spades; tear open all the envelopes and scatter all the papers lying peacefully inside them all over the house; stuff firewood under the blankets. And then, when her eyes had had their fill of these scenes of total destruction, she would return everything lovingly to its rightful place, exactly as it had been before.

One day, without really realizing what she was doing, Vaya started playing with fire. She selected one drawer for the purpose of relieving her compulsion, opened it, taking her time to study the contents carefully. After taking a deep breath, she started emptying it out. The she got up, went to the kitchen, gulped down a glass of chilled cherry juice and returned refreshed to the drawer. She meticulously put everything back in its place. It was all so easy; in a matter of minutes she had restored the drawer to its original state.

That was only the beginning. After the desk drawer there were other drawers, cabinets and cupboards, until not one corner of the house remained unexposed to the light of day, revealing objects which had been sealed away for years. It was not curiosity that drove her to go through his things; it was the joy at penetrating the holy of holies. Besides, she wasn't really interested in what was hidden away, in finding out what all those secret places concealed – and God forbid that she would ever steal anything. What she wanted was to disturb the prevailing order and destroy the illusion of tidiness, if only briefly. Then she would gather up the scattered objects without leaving a shred of evidence behind her. It was a game involving – no, demanding – everything a self-respecting game should include: good memory, sharp powers of observation, and that special ability to penetrate the unique way each person has of tidying up their things and leaving an imprint of themselves on it. What made the game particularly exciting for Vaya however was the sense of danger, in the same way that watching the stunts of acrobats takes on a new level of interest when the safety net is removed. There was no real danger that she would plunge headlong to the floor, but she knew that she and her trunks could easily end up on the streets again. It was the only thing Rodakis was strict about, and if he threw her out, he would be well within his rights – and she knew it.

One lovely morning, she opened the lower door of the old dresser. It stood away from the light under the stairs leading to the upper floor. It gave the impression that it was biding its time under there, secretively hatching some sinister plot. That area was always dark, even when the bright sun was directly outside. The darkness did not stop Vaya from realizing immediately that she had struck gold; gold after all glisters metaphorically too.

The things inside the dresser had not simply been stored there, they were on display, things of value to be admired which had been arranged in such a way that even a museum curator would have been impressed. Six engraved bone spoons arranged in the shape of a fan; a round wooden box with a lion's head for a lid; a pair of porcelain cups with pictures of dragons fired into them; a book bound in soft leather with a picture of an apple tree tooled into it; a crystal doorknob shaped like a highly polished diamond; a rosary of ivory beads; a blue glass, and other objects all put together to make up the picture of this hidden landscape.

Inside the box with the lion's head she found a small piece of paper folded double. There was a picture of a pyramid printed at the top, flanked by two words, foreign words. She recognized Rodakis's handwriting underneath. It said:

'Dry, Sweet, Bitter –
Proportions – after tasting –
Surround with smoke (if necessary).'

The bad weather persisted for a fortnight. Rain, hailstones and strong winds alternated constantly, and such low temperatures were unheard of on the island. Rodakis informed Paschalis that they would have to stop work until the weather improved, as it was quite impossible to work in these conditions. Paschalis was not happy. There was still a considerable debt on his sister's vineyards, but he appreciated that the matter was out of his employer's hands.

Enforced incarceration did not bring the two occupants closer together. They spent the better part of the day alone, shut away in their respective rooms while harrowing thunderclaps startled them both at irregular intervals.

On the morning of the ninth day, he found an unsigned note slipped under his door. It read: *I've trapped some birds. If you want, we can eat them together.*

He dressed and went downstairs. She was in the kitchen busy plucking various small birds: sparrows as well as some other larger ones, the bodies of which were piled up in a large metal bowl.

The moment she saw him, she repeated the message of her note verbatim.

'I've trapped some birds. If you want, we can eat them together.' He told her that he would be glad to join her and suggested they eat in the dining room instead of the kitchen. Then he left, asking her to let him know when they were ready.

The dining room, unlike the kitchen, was always dark. Long and narrow with a north-facing window at one end, the little light that did come through was muted by the presence of the loquat tree directly outside. It wasn't just recently that the room had fallen into disuse; it had never known any great moments.

By the time the house was built, its mistress was already dead, so there were never any real expectations that it would ever function as a proper dining room. There were a few notable exceptions, such as the occasion of Rodakis's sister's engagement. It was always closed up, more a reflection of the financial ease of a family whose honey business was at its peak than a room with any real practical function. The attenuated dull light from the sky, refracted through the foliage of the loquat, cast an indefinable green shade over the room.

The birds were presented on a deep serving dish, swimming in a runny red sauce, enough to feed at least six people. Vaya sat opposite Rodakis. They helped themselves; Vaya's special touch wasn't missing from this meal either, the personal stamp she put on everything she cooked.

'Perhaps it's the wood?' she answered when he put it to her.

'Wood? What wood?'

'I always put a piece of wood in the saucepan when I cook birds – pine or cypress. Never heard of that?'

She had a tendency to consider self-evident things that other people had never even heard of.

'No. Never.'

'That's because you're not a woman and you don't cook.'

Rodakis looked sceptical, but her argument floored him nonetheless.

'Where did you learn how to cook?' he asked her.

'Taught myself. Nobody needs to teach you. You learn by tasting and smelling. I've been cooking since I was very young.'

'It's delicious.'

'I caught a couple of thrushes too. My father taught me how to catch birds. With sticks.'

This was followed by a few moments of silence. Rodakis pulled the bones off a bird while Vaya carefully transferred some sauce onto her plate with a spoon. She stood up suddenly, as though anxious about something. He looked at her questioningly. She sat down again. A second later she was on her feet again, more composed this time, and walked towards the door, saying:

'I won't be long. Excuse me.'

Rodakis was so absorbed in the delicious bird flesh with the subtle aroma of cypress that he did not really register her absence. She was soon back.

'All right,' she said and sat down.

'All right,' he answered.

They continued their meal in silence. Her voice was heard later on, somewhat scrambled by her chewing.

'You haven't asked me anything.'

'What about?'

'Me. Who I am. Where I come from. What I'm doing on your island.'

'I haven't asked because I am not curious. And I don't want you to think that I wasn't going to let you into my house until I'd interrogated you. This is not a court of law.'

'I wish everybody thought like that.'

'How would I know if you were telling truth, anyway? You could say anything that came into your head, so what was the point of asking?'

'You're right. I probably would have lied,' she said with disarming honesty.

'You've got a limp.'

'Yes. I have. My right foot –' she paused, 'is not whole.'

Rodakis felt that he had been indiscreet and said, with slight embarrassment:

'You cook very well.'

'I don't mind,' she reassured him. 'A couple of years ago I lost a section of my foot, from the toes and a bit higher up. A human being did that to me.'

She rose to clear the table. Three birds were left on the serving dish, headless, with their legs sticking up in the air. She made two or three trips to the kitchen and back before the table was completely clear. Rodakis wondered if the time had not come to go up to his room. He decided to stay a while longer.

Vaya came back, carrying a bottle and a couple of glasses.

'I want you to try something,' she said and filled the first glass with the orange-coloured drink from the bottle.

'What is it?'

'It's made from loquats. You've got some out there,' she said, pointing to the tree outside the window, which was getting a good thrashing from the wind.

She filled her own glass, sat down opposite him again until dusk finally gave way to total darkness, and started to talk about her past.

Some people are proud of their past; others embarrassed by it; some people are indifferent to it, while for others, the past is so important that they spend more time planning it than they do planning the future. Around the time when he made the decision to sell off the land he had inherited to finance his round-the-world trip, he did very little beyond mapping out what would become his past in the future.

The time leading up to his departure (when his trip was still in the future) required a certain amount of organization, and was a joyless period. He had to find a buyer for the land, secure a good sale, make all the necessary arrangements, and above all, overcome the debilitating diffidence which made him lose his nerve whenever he was faced with something as ambitious as this, and which would wake him, bathed in sweat, from his nightmares.

The journey itself (the present) also had joyless moments in store: the endless searching for accommodation; the problem of communication; fear of local epidemics, and the never-ending changes in climate.

It was only when he returned to the island, unlocked the door to his house, went inside and unpacked that he started to derive any real pleasure from his long journey, especially as he set out his precious souvenirs inside the cupboard, thus filing away all his memories – the journey as past. His aim had been fulfilled – he had succeeded in creating a valuable past for his future. The only thing he needed now was to sit down in a comfortable chair and give himself up to his memories, fondling one of his precious souvenirs in the palm of his hand as he did so. All the images, sounds, landscapes, smells and faces he had encountered on his travels duly came to life. If there had been some way, some kind of magical intervention that would have enabled him to chalk up all these experiences from his travels without demanding any action on his part, he would never have left his armchair, and he would have been spared a lot of trouble too.

It was beyond Vaya how anyone could do something for the sole purpose of enriching his or her past. Her own past was something she didn't like to think about, and, given half a chance, would happily erase from her memory. She had adopted the tactic of selecting those aspects of her turbulent history which would best serve her purposes when trying to promote an image of herself designed to suit the circumstances, remaining mute on certain other points that might compromise this image. Thus the version the priest heard in confession was not the same as the one Rodakis heard that evening over the sound of falling rain.

Her narrative did not follow a chronological sequence; it jumped from one place to another, taking in various people without first explaining who they were or how they fitted in (Vaya typically considered everything to be self-evident). He occasionally interrupted her, asking for clarification, but she was so caught up in the whirl of reminiscences that she did not hear him – or at least gave that impression. Rodakis was unable to make sense of anything, and with each attempt he made to connect the scattered pieces of information into a coherent whole, he came up against a void.

Taking the facts he had gleaned to bed with him, he continued his attempt to discipline them into a cogent narrative, rehashing them, again and again, and failing, again and again. Eventually, he fell asleep, but even then he could not get Vaya out of his mind and recurring, jumbled images from her story filled his dreams.

Thunder woke him on three occasions. Each time he told himself to stop dreaming about her, especially at the moment when her husband was hacking off her foot with a spade. It was no use – the dreams persisted 'til morning. So did the rain. Four days of bad weather remained.

After she discovered the piece of paper in the box with the lion's head she was frequently tempted to ask Rodakis what the writing on it meant, but she never dared because she could not come up with a plausible explanation of how she knew about it in the first place. She made a number of attempts to interpret it, but without success. 'Dry, sweet, bitter – proportions after tasting,' read a bit like a recipe, or instructions for compounding some medicine or other curative substance, even though there was no mention of any particular ingredient. What made the thing so puzzling was the third phrase, 'Surround with smoke (if necessary).' If her faith in Rodakis as a rational human being was not so unshakeable, she might have started to wonder whether these slogans did not contain some kind of magic spell, or were somehow related to witchcraft.

She did not have to wait long for an answer. But before that, it was her turn to have one of her secrets revealed, one which she had kept to herself with remarkable resourcefulness. One bright moonlit evening, Rodakis was sleeping soundly, exhausted by the hard work which had resumed as soon as the weather had improved. He was woken abruptly by an unpleasant sensation, one which regularly shocked him out of sleep in the middle of the night: it felt as though a hand was cutting off his oxygen supply and pushing him to the verge of suffocation. He sat up and took a series of deep breaths, as deep as he could, rapid, asthmatic, like a dog that has been running around for hours in the sun on the hottest day of the year. He put it down to his sleeping position, which was clearly interfering with his breathing. The first few times it happened he was terrified, but he later acquired sufficient faith to believe that he would always wake up in time to stop himself from dying of suffocation.

He got up to open the window to inhale some fresh air. But the window, already warped after the recent rains, was impossible to open. He threw a blanket over his shoulders, slipped his feet into his shoes without tying the laces and crept downstairs as noiselessly as he could lest he wake Vaya, and went outside.

The beauty of the night landscape was disarming; the only sad thing was that the bright moonlight neutralized the gleam of the stars. He walked across the flat stones he had put down so that people's legs wouldn't get muddy, filling up his lungs with satisfying quantities of cold air as he went. The sea in the distance. Owls in the trees.

In two hours' time he would have to head off for work, and he wondered if it would be wiser to stay awake or to try to get some more sleep. Deciding on the latter, he turned round and headed back. The house was whitewashed by the moonlight, its irregular mass illuminated in the darkness.

Built at the peak of the honey business, it stood apart from the other houses on the island. For a start, the many recesses and projections created by the walls made it look like a tower constructed by a child using toy blocks. The inspiration behind it had been an Italian architect, passing through the island at the time on a tour of ancient sites. S. Rodakis who, with his newly acquired wealth, explicitly commissioned a house that would bear no trace of traditional island architecture, enlisted him. The Italian handed him the plans a few days later and left. S. Rodakis entrusted the building work to the local builders, who made a point of cursing Italy, ancient sites and honey on a daily basis. Nevertheless, they finished the job, and the result was indeed unconventional – just as S. Rodakis had ordered. As for the aesthetics, opinions differed.

When the house was ready, S. Rodakis decided that he needed some extra storage space for his gardening tools, something with an independent entrance to make it more functional. So he added on a structure to the main building, a large, long room – built with his own hands. Not surprisingly, it completely destroyed the harmony of the original plans. This room became the so-called back storeroom in which Rodakis put Vaya's trunks, a storeroom, which was never really used, despite the urgency with which it had been built.

He was not far from the house when he saw the protrusion of the storeroom. For the first time since Vaya had installed her worldly goods there, he started to wonder what was inside her two trunks; he didn't necessarily want to open them and go through them – just have a look. He was startled to find himself unable to open the door, a door that was always left unlocked; he didn't even have a key. He went round to the other side where there was a small window, permanently closed, but now open. He had the impression that there was a dim light coming from the inside but the moonlight made it difficult for him to be sure. He would need to get closer and take a look inside.

He brought his face up to the gap between the shutters. He was right. There was light in the room. Across from where he was standing, he could make out some rickety old chairs, rusty pieces of corrugated iron, desiccated branches, buckets of dried up paint, and various other building materials. He turned his head to the left, and pushing his head as far as the narrow gap would permit, his eyes rested on the two trunks. One was open. Vaya was bending over it with her back turned to him. She was obviously doing something, but from where he was standing it was impossible to tell what that something was. All he could see was the movements of her arms, working away intensely as though she were kneading dough, or folding laundry, or winding wool.

'At this time of night?' he asked himself. 'What on earth could she be doing in there at this hour?'

He sensed that whatever it was she was doing, she was doing it covertly, but he could not imagine why: if she wanted to do something in secret, why didn't she do it during the day when she had the house to herself?

A sudden movement interrupted this train of thought. Vaya lifted the contents of the trunk up with both arms, raising it high up above her head, in the way a mother would hold up a baby.

He summoned the courage to push his head right through the window to get a better look. Yes. It was a baby, a small, thin baby.

'What did you expect?' answered Father Chryssanthos apologetically, all the while scratching away at a drop of candle wax that had solidified on the sleeve of his cassock. 'My hands were tied. A confession is a confession.'

This was Rodakis's second visit to the priest. The first visit had been made three months earlier when he wanted to find out what was being done to find a family for Vaya to go and work for, as planned. The priest told him to be patient. However, on this occasion, Rodakis was not best pleased: both his words and the curl in his upper lip reflected his displeasure.

'What was I supposed to do?' he repeated, 'Betray the seal of confession? Come running to you saying, "Guess what? She's got a baby in one of those trunks!"'

'How does it manage to breathe inside there?'

'She doesn't keep it in there all the time. When you're out at work, she takes it out, and then in the evening she goes down and puts it to sleep in there, like a little bed. The infant is fine. There's no need to worry. And there's no danger of its falling out.'

'Why hasn't she told me about it? That's what I don't understand. I'd have had even more reason to let her stay if I'd known there was a baby.'

'She didn't want to. They're after her. The baby would give her away, don't you see? They're looking for a woman with a baby.

That's why I couldn't leave her anywhere else. She could never keep a baby hidden in an ordinary house – she didn't manage here for long. She was going to tell you. Really. She just needed to make sure she could trust you first. Anyway, the baby won't be a baby forever; she couldn't have kept it secret much longer.'

'You say they're after her.'

'I'm bound by her confession, please don't make me say any more. Hasn't she said anything to you?'

'She has. But nothing about doing anything that would make people come after her. She said she'd left home to escape a violent husband – the one who took her foot off with a spade.'

'Like I said – my hands are tied.'

'Has she been lying to me?'

'As God is my witness, I can't begin to tell what's true and what's not in all of this. The only thing that matters is that is our duty to help this poor, unfortunate creature.'

The priest was right. Rodakis was glad to help. He kissed the elderly priest's hand and left. On the way home, he did some thinking.

Why were they after her? What had she done? He recalled the words of the priest that first time: 'I can't put her in with the orphans in case anything gets into her during the night.' He knew at the time that this was no idle comment. One thing he was sure of, whatever it was that Vaya had or had not done, he was in no danger from her. He remembered how frightened he had been of her at first. All that seemed so distant now – and so comical.

And the baby? It explained a great deal: Vaya's isolation, in the beginning especially, and, even after a relationship of sorts had developed between them, she never seemed willing to let go of the sanctuary of the four walls of her room. Her sudden disappearances – that mealtime with the birds – all of this seemed perfectly logical now in light of the baby. His next thought stopped him dead in his tracks, looking blankly up at a bush on the roadside. That crying sound that he thought he'd heard

– he had attributed it to his hallucinations. He plucked a leaf off the bush. The priest, who'd been so anxious to arrange for the milkman to deliver milk to the house. He walked on. Her anxiety over finding the just the right place to store those trunks, as though they contained something valuable.

He hadn't told her that he knew about her secret. She, for her part, thought that Rodakis had no idea about the baby. But he couldn't let this go on.

As soon as the house came into view he resolved to bring it out into the open and have a frank discussion with her. She was digging up vegetables when he found her. He went up to her and said as plainly as possible:

'I know about your child. You can talk to me. Don't worry; you can trust me.'

At first she just stood there, refusing to understand the meaning of the words he spoke, as though he were speaking to her in some foreign language. When his words finally sank in, she was unable to speak. Eventually she regained possession of herself and answered just as plainly, though a tone lower:

'Let's go inside. Come on. I'll tell you everything.'

Most of the northern part of the island was sparsely populated even before the great fire. Rodakis's land, moreover, was the most isolated; apart from lying at some distance from the nearest houses, there was also a small hill on one side and a dry riverbed on the other, serving as natural boundaries. In view of this, Vaya's precaution of lowering her voice and closing the dining room door behind her in a remote place like this was pointless, but perhaps understandable in someone about to confide their secrets. They sat down on two of the dining chairs with roses carved into the wood, while the loquat drank up the last of the evening sunlight. The light was about to fade and the room would soon be dark, but that detail did not concern either of them just then. It did not seem to concern them even when it did get dark and their pupils had to strain through the murky light to see each other.

She talked about two men. The first was her husband. She said she had fallen in love with him, at least she thought she had, for his voice, his handsome eyebrows, and his strong fingers. Minor virtues, thought Rodakis – an inadequate foundation for a marriage. She soon realized that the man she had married was a spineless, incompetent creature whose only show of strength lay in the brutality of the beatings he gave her. This much he already knew, more or less. But what he didn't know was whether these acts of violence were entirely unprovoked.

'Was there a reason why he treated you like that?' he asked.

Weaving her fingers together she said nothing for a time and just stared down at them. She parted her lips without making a sound, but obviously intended to say something. After briefly gathering her thoughts, she started to talk about a second man.

Her father-in-law was a sailor. He had tried his best to attend his son's wedding but terrible storms had left him stranded somewhere in Africa. He arrived a month later, laden with exotic gifts. He spent six months with the newly-weds until it was time for him to leave again on another voyage. He enjoyed spending money and often invited the couple to go out and have fun with him. What was striking was how much the son resembled the father, physically at least. Her father-in-law had all the features that had first drawn her to her husband, only they sat much better on him. His eyes had the same beautiful shape, the same unusual colour, as well as a liveliness she never saw in her husband's vacant gaze. His eyebrows made the same attractive arched line, except that he did not wear a bad-tempered frown all the time, his fingers were strong too, but they were also amazingly nimble. They both had beautiful voices, rich and deep, and so alike that if you were blindfolded, you would never be able to tell them apart – except for the fact that one of them talked of distant lands full of panthers and enormous waterfalls, where the sun never set, while the other was content to chat about the idiots he had for friends and their inane practical jokes.

The six months the father spent with the couple were fateful. When Vaya looked at the man she married, all she could see was a cheap imitation of his father, a pitiful, failed second edition. He couldn't even carry off his good features; it was as though they really belonged on his father and he had come by them through some blind hereditary system, without deserving them; without being entitled to them.

First it shocked her. Then it scared her: at first unconsciously but then filled with anxiety, she'd count the days 'til the ship would set sail and take the original away with it, leaving her with the copy. Time was precious. Time was torture.

She tried to find excuses to pamper him and make a fuss of him with small, invisible acts of devotion. She placed sprigs of rosemary and lavender in the pockets of his freshly laundered clothes; she made sure that the water in the glass on his bedside cabinet was always cool, she would serve him the best cuts of meat and save the ripest fruits for him; gaze at him furtively and 'accidentally' brush past him. All of this was punctuated with stomach pains and unprovoked fits of melancholy.

'As for the other one, he wasn't exactly blind,' she said, referring to her husband. 'There may have been a lot wrong with him, but he knew exactly what was going on.'

Despite the fact that she never admitted to this secret passion when her husband confronted her with it, she bore his vengeful violence in silence. She bore it and felt that it was deserved (despite what she said to the contrary) because she looked on it as a way of paying for part of the sin weighing down on her. His bad treatment of her continued unabated even after his father's departure, and was firmly rooted in the couple's mutual belief that the situation merited such measures.

Then the letters started. She wrote to him almost every day, but her letters remained unsent. She hid them inside a pillowcase and eventually sent them off all together, to the hotel in Alexandria from which he had sent them a postcard, telling them that he would be staying there for a while longer. There were thirty-three letters. She arranged them in chronological order, wrapped them up in thick grey paper and copied the address of the hotel from the postcard. She felt like a murderer who, after carefully preparing the ground, finally commits the crime.

The first letters were reserved, brief, and formal. In the next batch she allowed a small cloud to gather, gradually casting a shadow over the couple's life. She assumed all the responsibility, saying that she was not worthy of the good man she had married, but she did not explain the root of the problem. However, in letter twenty-nine everything came pouring out in a delirious outburst. This was followed by a further four letters of desperate love. It was then when the postcard from Alexandria suddenly arrived. She stopped writing and posted the thirty-three letters she had written. Then she waited. For what, she did not know, but she waited all the same.

If she had sent the letters, one by one, in the order they had been written, he would have seen the progression towards the climax. But he received them all at once, and the mere bulk of the package overwhelmed him with anxiety and bewilderment. His postcard contained no more than thirty words; she had answered with over thirty letters. Rodakis eventually got up to turn the light on, and asked:

'Did he answer you?'

'No. He didn't. And then he disappeared. It was a while before there was any sign of life from him. My husband worried about his father, worried something had happened to him. Of course I knew that he hadn't drowned or anything like that. I knew why he wasn't in touch. Then we got a telegram, just to let us know that he was all right.'

'Didn't you see him again?'

'Yes, I did. But a long time afterwards, a long, long time. A year and a half ago, well, a year and seven months, he turned up on the doorstep, out of the blue. First thing he said to me was, "You ought to be ashamed of yourself!" '

'Wasn't the other one at home?'

'No. He wasn't. He knew his son would be out. That's why he came. He'd been waiting for him to leave the house.'

At this point, Vaya broke off. She simply sat and stared at the table. Insects drawn to the light congregated at the window. Eventually Rodakis asked her:

'Did he insult you?'

'Yes. Called me a contemptible whore who didn't have any respect for anything – said I was on a path to perdition, and the sooner I got there the better. And plenty more besides. Cruel words. Horrible insults. But all the time his hands were all over me, caressing me, messing up my clothes. Then he threw me to the floor, and stopped cursing. Started kissing me, and then got up to unbuckle his belt, and said that I was damned. He threw himself down on top of me again and didn't say anything else 'til he'd finished. Then he called me a filthy slut again and left, slamming the door behind him. He was back the next day. And the day after. He'd come as soon as the other one left for work. But those other two times he didn't curse me; he didn't even speak to me. He just threw himself on top of me. Didn't even say good-bye on his way out. Nothing. I never saw him again.'

The insects were looking in through the window, motionless and silent, like a theatre audience, breathless before the climax of the action. Vaya continued.

'He sent me a letter, to my cousin Nectaria's (I'd told him that he could use her address if he wanted to write), about three months later, returning the thirty-three letters I'd written to him. He wrote to me as if nothing had ever happened, as though there had never been those three times. He said he was returning my letters – listen to this – so that I could destroy them myself, with my own two hands, and feel that I was killing off the sickness inside me. I realized then that he was in fact much worse than his son. After all, his son had some justification for thinking and acting the way he did, and though he might not have been anything special, he was at least honest and straight. He wasn't wicked or devious like his father. Those three times, which should have been so happy for me – I'd have tried to forget about them if they hadn't given me my daughter.'

'Your baby,' asked Rodakis gently, 'she's a girl?'

'Yes. That's right. My little Rosa.'

They both turned their heads towards the window at the same time; a large brown moth had crashed into the windowpane with a loud thud.

Two wooden bookcases stood on opposite walls in the big room. S. Rodakis, a true bibliophile, had bought most of the books. He was not a particularly avid reader but he found the idea of bringing together the sum of centuries of human knowledge into one room profoundly moving. Human knowledge – that was what charmed him. Literature, on the other hand, left him indifferent; he considered it to be a fraud and the luxury of the leisured classes. For many years he corresponded with the owner of one of the capital's largest bookshops, who kept him up to date with new publications and would send out anything S. Rodakis ordered on the first boat. A large number of these titles were foreign, French mostly, condemned in advance to suffer the harshest fate a book could have – to remain unread. Nobody in the house knew any foreign languages. S. Rodakis reasoned that this in no way detracted from the value of the works in question which safeguarded the supreme good – human knowledge – in their pages. His eyes fell lovingly over the titles of weighty tomes such as *Astronomie, Exercises de géométrie, L'Art ferrarais à l'époque des princes d'Este* as they stood there, erect as headstones, lined up on the shelves, holding a vast body of obscure information.

E. Rodakis, Rodakis's sister, disliked books. She thought that anyone who spent time on books had to be either very old or very odd. As a girl, she often dreamt that she went downstairs and ripped out the pages from the books one by one and listened to them as they howled in pain. This was the reason why Rodakis was so startled when she asked if she could borrow his botany book – she claimed that she wanted to use the design on the front cover for an embroidery pattern.

Until a certain age, Rodakis was indifferent to the contents of the ever-increasing burden on the bookshelves. Later, his interest was sparked by one particular title. It was a book on geology, and was about caves. This was the book that first exposed him to the secret pleasures of reading, which, like his father before him, he inevitably connected exclusively with the natural sciences. The next step was for him to develop a deep contempt for light reading, again just like his father, especially for novels dealing with the affairs of the heart. Naturally he only ever heard about such novels, and never read one himself. Nevertheless, he considered them to belong to the most despicable of genres. Moreoever, his aversion to romantic literature coloured his view of love to a great extent.

So as Vaya sat in semi-darkness unravelling the threads of her shady past, Rodakis was worried that he would get caught up in reminiscences of a romantic tragedy and would have to endure all the bitterness and sexual anguish of a woman scorned, down to the very last drop. However, the neutral tone Vaya adopted – as though it had nothing to do with her personally – and the coolness in her voice, kept the potential for melodrama to a minimum. It was only when she got to the part about the thirty-three letters that Rodakis started to fidget and got up to turn the light on. At no point did he wish to bring his personal opinion to bear on what he was hearing, and restricted himself to asking questions only when he judged them necessary for the purpose of keeping the narrative on track. He was successful in this and found that he was able to follow her story. He was anxious for an opening to ask her the only thing which really bothered him about the whole business: who was after her and why?

The moth, which had startled them by crashing loudly into the windowpane briefly, ruptured the flow of her narrative, just long enough for him to put the question to her:

'Why are they after you?'

Judging by the slight twitch her face gave at this question, Rodakis realized that he had embarrassed her. Even so, she answered him immediately.

'One of those three times he came, it seems that he was seen. Someone went running to my husband and said that he must be happy to have his father back. I insisted that he must have mistaken him for the handyman who'd been over making some small repairs. He believed me. Not because he trusted me, but because he couldn't imagine that his own father would do such a thing behind his back. He didn't put it past me though. But later, when I got pregnant, he sat down and counted the months, and worked out that he couldn't be the father because when I got pregnant he hadn't been near me for ages on account of an infection – doctor's orders. So he put two and two together. That's when he got hold of the spade. He said he'd kill me one day, but was waiting for me to give birth to his brother and then he'd do it. 'I'll find you, wherever you go. I'll come after you and I'll kill you.' The minute he'd said it, he came at me with the spade and took my toes off with it. As soon as I could walk on it again, I threw some things together when he wasn't looking and went to my cousin Nectaria's house. I stayed with her for a bit. One day, before the baby was born, I heard her shouting for me to come downstairs. She'd just woken up and seen the words '*I will find you*' carved into her front door. Beautiful big capitals, obviously not done in a hurry – that was the frightening part. Like he was saying, I know where you are, I'll wait until the birth then I'll come after you and I'll kill you. Wonderful piece of craftsmanship;

must have hired someone to do it – that's the only explanation. People used to stop outside and admire it. I saw the way they looked at it.

'As soon as I saw those letters with all those twirls and curls I knew I was done for; the baby came early, probably because of the fright. It took me a couple of days to recover and then I left in the night. I had no idea where I was going. I had Rosa in the trunk, a bit of money in a small bag (which was stolen from me on the third day). I managed to sneak onto a ship. I just wanted to get as far away as possible but they made me get off when we were not even half way there because I couldn't pay for my ticket.'

'He'll never find you here,' said Rodakis, softly.

'I can't stay here forever.'

The confession had come to an end. Rodakis was pleased that she had confided in him and wanted to return the compliment by sharing something personal of his with her.

'Stand up,' he said.

'Why? What's going on?' she asked, more in surprise than anything else.

'Come with me. I want to show you something.'

She rose numbly to her feet and followed him through the dark house, searching for some indication of his intentions. He led her to the staircase. She was sure this uncertainty would last until they got upstairs. But he by-passed the staircase and squeezed himself into the corridor and into the empty space under the staircase, where the underside of the steps was visible, like a photographic negative or the reverse side of a piece of embroidery. This was where the dresser stood, as though lying in wait, hoping to frighten some unsuspecting victim as they walked past.

Rodakis unhooked a lantern from the wall and lit it.

'This is my cupboard of valuables,' he said as he bent down holding the lamp. 'It's a collection of objects I accumulated on a long journey.'

Vaya looked on with feigned surprise at the closed door, while a vivid picture of the exact contents of the interior flashed across her mind. She could swear that even now she could mess up and rearrange the objects in their correct position.

'Valuables?'

'Yes, because each one of these objects was brought back from far away, and now there are objects made in countries thousands of kilometres away from each other sitting here together in the same cupboard.'

His explanation was lost on her. She was preoccupied with the piece of paper with the incomprehensible writing on it.

'Do you want to have a look?'

She nodded, giving him the signal to turn the key. He opened the door slowly in order to prolong her anxiety to see what was inside. The hinges let out a pervasive squeak (which could have been avoided if he had opened it in the normal way). In the quivering light of the lantern, laid bare before them, was the still life of his collection.

'Well?'

'Beautiful. Very beautiful.'

She planned her next move.

'This is lovely,' she said, placing the box with the lion head lid in the palm of her hand. 'Where does it come from?'

'Egypt. In the foyer of my hotel there was a display case selling various souvenirs.'

'Nice carving,' she commented, stroking the lion's head with her fingertip above its open mouth and menacing teeth.

In one swift delicate move she removed the lid.

'There's a piece of paper in here,' she said handing over the folded sheet to Rodakis, looking him straight in the eye as she did so. He took it and unfolded it.

He cast a quick eye over it and said, 'Yes'.

She continued to look at him enquiringly, fully expecting an answer.

The image of Vaya's face, semi-illuminated in the lamp-light, fixing him with her insistent stare, a stare so intense that it even succeeded in casting a shadow over those colourless eyes of hers, scored itself on Rodakis's memory to such an extent that even after she had crossed over into the territory of the past, this memory of her, disembodied in time and space, always accompanied his recollections of her. He tried in vain to remember where and when the half-lit face with the determined stare had confronted him or what it was that it so hungrily demanded.

He had also forgotten how surprised he'd been by that same stare. It was natural that he should be, since Vaya never seemed the slightest bit curious and was never indiscreet. Not that he had noticed, anyway. As far as the contents of the notepaper were concerned, it was not that he regarded as personal. He just assumed that they would be of no interest to her, and that is what he told her.

'You wouldn't be interested.'

'You don't have to tell me,' she said, detaching her gaze from him.

'It's nothing secret; one of my father's strange ideas, one that came to him when was he was no longer of sound mind – shortly before his death.'

Vaya who had been puzzling endlessly over the meaning of these cryptic phrases was determined not to allow this heaven-sent opportunity to pass unexploited.

'What do you mean 'strange ideas'? – If you don't mind me asking, that is.'

'My father,' said Rodakis, his speech assuming the tones of a lecture, 'was a bee-keeper. At one stage we produced a great deal of honey. Until the fire. After that my father gave it up. (You need to know all this – it's important). One day after he had lost his mind, he took me to one side and said, "I'm looking for the formula." "What formula?" I asked him, thinking he meant a chemical formula because he was very interested in chemistry, even though he probably didn't understand half of what he read about it. But he was talking about something quite different. The formula he was trying to work out had to do with the plants the bees suck pollen from.'

'Yes, but what formula? I don't understand,' said Vaya, genuinely surprised.

'The correct formula – the right recipe, if you prefer. The one that would yield the best honey. That's what he was trying to discover. That's what he meant by "formula". You see, the taste of honey is determined by what the bees eat, what trees and flowers they gather nectar from. The ideal formula would be determined by the plants they ate. And in what proportions. He had divided flowers into three sub-categories: sweet smelling – like freesias or lilacs; bitter smelling – lemon blossom and bitter oranges; and dry scented, like thyme, reeds and pine flowers. The problem was how much of each the bees should have. That was what would govern the formula. You know, he had even developed a system of isolating the bees, closing off the area where the bees gathered nectar, with torches dug into the ground all around. The smoke would keep the bees inside the area and stop them straying to other plants and ruining the proportions.'

Nervous laughter intruded at the end of this explanation to give the impression that he was not being altogether serious – although it was clear that these were not his own words but the words of another person – an insane person at that.

Vaya did not join in with the laughter. She was thrilled that the riddle which had perplexed her for so long, firmly sealed behind the teeth of a mute sphinx, had finally been solved, and now stood naked and transparent before her like the air released by a burst bubble.

Later that evening he asked her to show him the baby. He followed her down to the storeroom. That was Rosa's last night in the trunk.

E. Rodakis was in a state of agitation. Once again, her brother was to blame.

It was truly remarkable: they led completely separate lives. They lived some distance away from each other and met only rarely (for example at the feast of the local saint, or the regular celebration down on the beach – and even then not necessarily every year). It was a wonder that each managed to constitute a permanent source of irritation for the other.

He embarrassed her; the fact that he was her brother embarrassed her even more. Why did that particular individual have to be her brother when there were any number of men on the island she would rather have had in his place? Men who would have made more normal brothers: men who, when she was little, would have plaited her hair for her, men whose comforting arms she would have rushed into at the slightest upset or fright. Or who at least would not have had hallucinations or ears that buzzed. Indeed, of all the men she knew of her bother's age, there was only a handful she considered to be inferior brother-material: there was that ex-convict, the deaf mute, and a few other difficult cases. Of course the fact that they lived so far away from each other made things much easier, but nothing and no one could change the reality that they were, and would remain, brother and sister. He would be her brother forever.

But the general fact of her brother's shortcomings was not responsible for her distress that day; its cause was more specific; it was that barely-concealed innuendo behind her neighbour's remark from the other side of the hedge:

'Your brother married, with a great big kid and everything, and you never said a word!'

In other circumstances she would have thought the woman was teasing her, or else had gone mad, but the unmistakable irony in her voice which penetrated the dense hedge, was confirmation enough that she had her facts straight.

So she had to endure this too, did she? Her brother going off, getting married and having a baby, without inviting her either to the wedding or her nephew's christening. The woman had said 'great big kid', hadn't she? So there must have been a christening at some point? Unless – even worse – there was a wife and a child without any church services surrounding them. No wedding. No christening. Nothing.

With this last speculation, her distress intensified to the point that she started pacing the floor nervously going from room to room, only stopping when, in a moment of distraction, she stubbed her little toe on the leg of the iron bed. She looked at the black metal full of hatred and would happily have turned round and kicked it if she hadn't worried about the pain, so she had to content herself with spitting at it: another terrible day in the life of E. Rodakis.

If all this was true, she really didn't know what else to expect. How could she forget all the unspeakable things he'd done to her in the past? How could she forget that trip he went on after their father's death, when everybody was asking her where her brother was, and she would have to bite her tongue, not having the slightest idea what to say. What could she say? That her brother had hastily sold off some land and left on a round-the-world trip? Any rational human being would have had him down as insane and she was only too aware of the fact that her family history could not easily accommodate another case of madness. At least he could have brought her back a special present, some jewellery, something hand-carved, some silver, a crocodile or snakeskin belt – like the one she had begged him to get for her on the ship just before he set sail. Seeing that her entreaties to make him cancel his trip were in vain, she thought she might at least get a belt out of it. But he didn't bring her anything. Nothing. Nothing at all. When she bumped into him in the street two days after his return, she asked him, completely naturally, if he had brought back anything nice from his travels. And he answered her, completely naturally, that he had bought a number of beautiful souvenirs, including an illustrated book on botany, which he promptly produced from one of his pockets to show her. There was no mention of a belt.

There were countless other examples of his frivolity. A short while before, she had been informed (again by a third party) that he had decided to change his profession again, had given up being a builder (which as far she could tell was very lucrative), and had taken up his father's old profession of bee-keeping. Naturally, the decision itself was of no interest to her; it was just typical of the ridiculous way he approached everything in life.

The business of the wife and child was different. The question of whether her brother had actually married, and if he had a child, concerned her directly, and she should have been told. She decided to go and find out for herself.

She set off for her childhood home at night, on foot. Her intention was to get there by dawn so that there would be just enough light for her to see what was going on inside the house, but not enough for her to be spotted. Her route forced her through some of the burnt section of the island. An excuse for a lantern lit her path; the darkness was impenetrable and its effects so pervasive that it cancelled out all initiative for thought. The only human feeling that could be experienced in such blackness was panic, that particular strain of panic the diver experiences as he enters an underwater tunnel, unsure about the oxygen in his lungs, and all he can think about is whether or not he will emerge alive. The only thing that wasn't black was the stars. And they were very high in the sky. It was as though some inscrutable force of nature had detached the flowers that once grew on those now charred trees, breaking them off their twigs and holding them suspended above her head. She also stumbled on the burnt remains of a wooden shack, probably some old hunters' shelter.

That was black too. Thoughts of her small terracotta flowerpots with their colourful petunias standing on white marble suddenly came to her and gave her courage.

At first light the house came into view. Her calculations had been right; she'd followed the course of the dry riverbed passing in front of it. Once in the garden, she dashed across to the old storeroom, relatively confident that she would manage to get round the house, wall by wall, from there, and take a look inside any windows that happened to be open.

The back window of the storeroom was closed – she hadn't been expecting to see anything particularly significant in there anyway. The next window was the dining room. Open. Nothing of interest in there. Next, the kitchen window.

'Rabbit!' she exclaimed. Standing by the sink was a bowl full of peeled vegetables.

Next window – their father's bedroom. Closed. Next, open. The big room. Everything was just as she remembered it; it was as though nothing had been touched by human hands since the day she left. But under the desk she could just about make out (as far as it was possible to see anything, because although the sun had sent out its first rays, the house was still dark), a piece of checked fabric, which definitely reminded her of something, but the intensity of the moment prevented it from coming to her. Next a small fanlight and then the two small sitting room windows, which were always kept shut.

She had already covered three of the four sides of the ground floor; that left the side with the front door and the window next to it. Carefully crouching down to have a look, she suddenly remembered that the gingham material she had seen was from a dress of one of her old rag dolls. She could now be sure of two things: a woman who cooks rabbit; a girl who plays with dolls. She had all the evidence she needed. All that was left was to decide how to take things from there. She turned round and made to leave.

She was on the last of the steps leading up to the front door when she heard it open behind her. The sound cut through her like a knife. She turned round and saw Rodakis looking at her with the expression of a startled carnivore.

'What do you want?' he asked her.

In the few seconds of silence that ensued she observed with horror that her mind was slowly but steadily emptying itself out, losing its special skill for coming up with good excuses on the spur of the moment, until somewhere in its deepest recesses the only excuse which could save her came to her. It was immediately obvious just how stupid and inappropriate it was, but at that moment it was her only safety net. She tried to think of something else, something more plausible, but the mounting pressure of her brother's gaze meant that she had to say something. And quickly.

'Your botany book.'

E. Rodakis did not discover the existence of the two new people in her brother's life until they had been living in his house for four years. A lot had happened during that time; important decisions had been taken.

First, Rodakis decided to play the role of father to Vaya's child, for at least the duration of their stay on the island. Despite the fact that the locals never seemed to pay much attention to what was going on in other people's lives (Rodakis even less than most), he nevertheless felt that by doing this, he would secure the protection and the cover they needed. The priest baptized the little girl Rodanthi, after Vaya's mother. The baptism was held at the house one wet sunny day.

The other important decision was that he left the building trade. The idea was originally to do so on a trial basis and to work as a bee-keeper, testing S. Rodakis's ideas to see if there was anything to them.

Vaya was active in the process that led to this decision. She imperceptibly sowed the germ of the idea in Rodakis's mind, that his deranged father's honey formula was perhaps not the product of dementia but an older idea that had lodged itself at the back of the old man's mind and perhaps would have involved some research which, after the fire, he had been unable to carry out. When Rodakis made the decision, she offered to assist him in the enterprise, and he accepted. This was what she had had in mind from the outset, as she desperately tried to come up with a way to stay on in his house.

Rodakis was confident that Vaya's help would prove invaluable. Quite apart from her extraordinary talent for experimenting with flavours, he would need practical help taking care of the bees. So each emerged feeling that they had weighted the agreement in their own favour.

As time went on, Rodakis grew accustomed to Vaya's presence in the house and would reflect how he enjoyed many of the privileges of a *pater familias* without ever getting entangled in the processes of matchmaking, quarrelling, passion, negotiations between families, tears and anger, as well as a whole host of obligations. He was completely independent; nobody was required to approve of or agree with his decisions. He had a vague fondness for Vaya. He respected the fact that she had never become a burden, and that in spite of her misfortune, she didn't wander around looking miserable, and she always carried out his wishes to the letter. In other respects, her presence in the house had gradually become indifferent to him, and she was no longer the bizarre creature of their first meeting. The little girl, on the other hand, was gaining more and more of his attention. He saw her as a wonderful opportunity to observe at first hand not only the development of the human body but also of human intelligence. He kept detailed records of the precise dates on which the slightest physical development was noticed, whether related to the growth of teeth, limbs, suppleness of the

joints, speech development and sentence structure, coordination, behaviour and reflexes.

At the same time he enlisted the other basic tool at the disposal of the researcher – the experiment. An issue that held endless fascination for him and was to become the subject of experimentation, was whether a small child has the same view of what is unpleasant (or at least not pleasant), as an adult.

For example, he would take the chamber pot which the child had just filled and place it close to her nose; while she played happily with her rag doll, he would creep up behind her and pour a cup of cold water over her head; he would hand her a piece of cheese with one of Vaya's coarse black hairs wrapped around it to eat. Needless to say, all these experiments were kept secret from the child's mother, and were conducted either when she was outside or was busy doing something else.

Like the afternoon when Vaya was in the garden burning leaves, confident that Rodakis was watching Rosa. For some reason, however, she came back into the house and into the kitchen where she witnessed the following scene: Rodakis was sitting on a chair. Sitting on the table facing him was Rosa. A plate with leftover aubergines from lunch was on the table. He opened his mouth, filled it, and chewed. But instead of swallowing, he stuck out his tongue with the mashed up food still on it. This procedure was repeated. Rosa just sat there looking at him distractedly. Now and again, with the help of a little water, he emitted tiny little (and not so tiny little) belches. One of these belches made Rosa giggle, at which he opened the blue book lying on the table next to him and jotted something down. Then he lifted her down and gave her an affectionate little smack.

Vaya slipped out of the kitchen quietly and returned to the supervision of the bonfire. The reflection of the flames flickered in her eyes together with the disturbing realization that the man she lived with was completely insane.

They constructed the first hives themselves out of large pieces of hollowed-out tree trunks.

But that was the least of their problems. They had to tackle much more serious difficulties before that. Decisions were made after several lengthy conferences in the dining room, which had established itself as the decision-making centre of the house. As for the site of the hives, they chose after considerable deliberation to set them up on the land Rodakis had inherited, the only part he had not sold off. While its small size was a disadvantage, it did belong to them, and its location was perfect, it was right in the heart of the burnt woodland, which would guarantee that the bees were isolated, in line with the requirements of the experiment.

One of the difficulties of the enterprise was that any adjustments they needed to make to the proportions of 'bitter, sweet and dry' had to wait a full year, that is until the following year's harvest. That fact made it clear that the time line for seeing results and drawing conclusions was too long. In view of this, Rodakis decided that irrespective of the progress of the experiment, they would sell whatever honey they had in order to secure at least some income. To that end, he set about constructing a makeshift sheltered stand, a kind of kiosk, at the entrance to the property. Glass jars were later displayed on it, and a bell was hung from the roof for customers to ring and alert them to their presence.

They bought bulbs, shrubs and saplings, which in their view covered all three categories – sweet, bitter and dry – and planted them in equal quantities. Nine days were spent knee-deep in soil. The ground was fertile and receptive, yielding willingly to their spades and eagerly accepting the roots of the plants it was fed, as though it realized that it was in its interest to cooperate. They started wearily in the morning and finished late at night. Not even the rain, which twice put in an appearance, could deter them; on the contrary, they greeted it as a positive sign and went on digging in the mud. On the last day they looked at each other in bewilderment.

They knew that they should not expect too much from the first year since their efforts were more experimental than anything, and it was still early days. Nevertheless, the first batch of honey was much better than they had dared hope, and the few people who heard that Rodakis was producing and selling honey and went up to buy a jar, soon came back for more, and spread the word to new customers too. They were the only strangers to have set foot on Rodakis's property for years.

Vaya never answered the bell. By now, almost everybody knew that Rodakis had a woman living in his house, but she preferred to keep out of sight. The same went for Rosa. When customers arrived, she made herself scarce. It didn't seem to bother her; it was just one of those things she had learned to take for granted, like eating at a table and sleeping in a bed. As soon as she spotted a head emerging over the horizon mounting the slope leading up to the house, she would run to hide in her mother's bedroom and stand and watch from the window and wait there until the customer left.

One day, however, it didn't work like that. Rosa was engrossed in a column of ants, which were trying to convey a dead grasshopper to its nest. By the time she heard the footsteps, it was too late. A woman wrapped in a red headscarf was approaching the entrance to the property, smiling at her the way adults do when they see a small child. Rosa, panic-stricken, turned and fled, dragging the lifeless body of the grasshopper along on her foot as she did. The woman's voice echoed behind her:

'And who do you belong to?'

Without waiting for an answer she marched in, heading straight for the stall. She stood there for a while, assuming that the little girl had gone to fetch somebody, but when nobody appeared, she rang the bell. Rodakis appeared without delay. The woman took her honey, put her money down on the stall, and asked:

'Who does the child belong to?'

He looked at her searchingly, with a look that concealed the exact same question, 'Yes, whose is she?' or perhaps, 'What do you want me to say?' That was the moment he made up his mind, if rather impulsively, without giving the matter much thought, to appear to the world as Rosa's father.

'She's mine,' he said with determination in his voice.

The woman turned on her heels and left, muttering as she went 'a long life to her'.

As soon as the woman was out of sight, he put his hands up to his forehead and whispered something Vaya, when she saw him through the window, could not hear. Something told her it was serious and somehow connected with Rosa's recent appearance: she had burst into the house in tears, refusing to explain why. Vaya abandoned the child to her sobbing and ran breathlessly into the garden, prepared for the worst.

He hadn't moved. He was still holding his head in his hands. When he saw her, instead of speaking to her, he started walking up to the house. She realized that she was supposed to follow him. They went into the dining room and closed the door.

'I've made a decision,' said Rodakis, in a voice so grave it was almost funereal.

Vaya feared that he was about to tell her to pack her things and leave.

'I'm going to acknowledge your daughter as my own. The child can't go on living hidden away like this. Nobody knows how long we're going to carry on living together. Perhaps next year when we change the proportions we'll achieve what we have set out to achieve. But it might take two, three years even. Is the child to stay hidden away all that time? Like she is now? No, this has been going on long enough!'

Her lips were as straight and closed as they had been before she heard this announcement; if she let down her guard, they would have settled into an enormous smile, creating a perfect semi-circle.

Her joy was twofold: on the one hand there was the relief that yet again the threat of finding herself on the streets had failed to materialize, and on the other hand, this new situation gave her the perfect cover; even if her worst nightmare did come true, and her husband suddenly appeared on the island looking for her, asking all and sundry if they'd seen a woman with a limp carrying a child in her arms, even then, Rosa would no longer be the unknown child of a strange woman and an even more obscure father. She was the daughter of Rodakis, a man from one of the island's oldest families, almost as old as its ancient ruins. And people would put their quiet, reclusive existence down to Rodakis's eccentric personality, rather than suspect there was anything strange about her. In a flash, everything became clear to Vaya: until that moment, she had never been able to get the image of the exquisite lettering of the phrase '*I will find you*' out of her mind.

'I think it's best for everybody, especially the child.' Rodakis was still pursuing his own line of thought.

'I agree,' said Vaya, accommodatingly.

Rodakis brought the discussion to a close with an emphatic, 'That's it, then'.

'But…' Vaya was just in time to stop him on his way out. 'What's my place in all this now?'

'You are the child's mother.'

'I am the child's mother. You are the child's father. That means we are…'

'Man and wife,' exclaimed Rodakis. 'In the eyes of the world we are man and wife. Goodbye.'

His cold farewell was designed to make it clear that nothing had changed between them, and their status of man and wife existed solely for the benefit of other people. Besides, it was quite unnecessary for him to say goodbye; after all, he was only going into the garden.

Once alone, Vaya was free to smile, free to let herself go. She could finally look to the future with optimism. She stood up and hurried to her room, and dug out a bottle containing something strong – it was almost pure alcohol. Just as she was extracting the cork with her teeth, she heard a small sob and saw Rosa sitting on the floor, her back half leaning against the wall, the other half pressed against the iron bedstead. She had stopped crying but the occasional involuntary sob escaped up through her throat. Vaya reclined on the bed, and gulped down her first big swig, abandoning herself to the vapours of happiness enveloping her.

At the next little sob she turned her head and said:

'What are you still crying for, silly?'

When Rodakis decided to leave the building trade he did so with an easy heart. Despite his natural bent for the work, he never believed that he was cut out for the job. But he had to tie up a loose end: Paschalis. He knew how much the young man was counting on the income he got from working alongside him, and this made it hard for him to break the news; but it couldn't be helped.

He wondered how he had suddenly acquired so many dependants – it was almost as if fate had pushed them in his direction until they were huddled round him claiming his protection, at a time when he had not properly determined his own path in life. It was some consolation that he had managed to get rid of his sister; that was important. But in her place not one but three heads had sprung up.

Paschalis took the news harder than expected. At first he just listened with his head hung low, and when Rodakis got to the end of his short announcement, he looked up and shook his head, slowly, left and right, with an expression full of bitterness and with as much contempt as one human being could feel towards another.

'I can imagine what sort of problems this news creates for you,' said Rodakis, taking a step closer to him. 'But do try to understand that there comes a time in all our lives when decisions have to be made. And there are times when we have to make those decisions very quickly, without giving them a lot of thought. But we still make them, because at the time we think we are doing the right thing. And that's the case with me – I had to decide whether I wanted to be a builder for the rest of my life. I can assure you (and I hope you'll take me at my word), my only regret in all this is you. I am not an unfeeling man; I know that you need the money – never mind that the reason is not one I can sympathise with. Whatever the case, please understand that I cannot organise my life around other people's debts. Especially when I have the opportunity to apply myself to something that requires research and study, and which, if successful, will mean that I have made a breakthrough of sorts. And if it fails, I won't have lost anything – on the contrary, I will have a much less tiring job, there's no comparison, even if it means making less money. I'm not trying to justify myself; I really don't think I have to; I would just like it if you could understand that things have changed and that you had better look elsewhere for work. Of course this means that I – '

As he launched into his last sentence, Rodakis took a further step towards Paschalis and stretched out his hand to touch his shoulder, but as soon as his hand made contact, Paschalis brushed him off violently, his eyes blazing, thus bring the unfinished sentence to a halt

'That's right. Look elsewhere. Assuming that I don't work for the fun of it – I do need money – so I'll look elsewhere for work. Thanks for the advice. If in the meantime my sister is out on the streets, what do you care? Just as long as your precious research goes well. I'd like to see you in my shoes, watching your sister with a noose around her neck.'

'It wouldn't distress me unduly if I did.'

'That's because you're an unfeeling pig.'

Rodakis, who was not an irascible man and only ever lost his temper when people interfered with his possessions, overlooked his young assistant's impertinence; anyway, he still liked him and although he did not feel in the least guilty about it, he could understand the despair his sudden announcement must have caused. He tried to pick up the broken thread of his last sentence, the one he had started before Paschalis had pushed him off so abruptly. If he had let him finish, he would have seen that his employer was willing to tide him over until he found work. But Rodakis repeated the mistake of beginning with the same phrase, 'I was thinking,' and once again tried to rest his hand on Paschalis's shoulder, and Paschalis repeated the mistake of interrupting him and pushing him away. Consequently, Rodakis's offer of help was never made.

The second time he brushed his employer's hand off, Paschalis felt strangely elated, experiencing a rush of sweetness which fuelled a desire to keep pushing Rodakis until he gave such a forceful push that he was sent stumbling two or three paces back in an effort to prevent himself from falling. They both paused. Rodakis looked at Paschalis, nonplussed and Paschalis felt a primitive instinct welling up inside him.

A second push sent Rodakis to the ground. By the time he realised what had happened, Paschalis was moving towards him. He stopped, straddled him and then lowered himself down onto Rodakis's stomach, squeezing the man's ribcage so tightly between his thighs that he could hardly breathe. Looking up at the young man bearing down on him like that, like some enlarged distortion of his normal self, Rodakis was worried that Paschalis had taken leave of his senses, and feared that in this state it wouldn't take much for him to kill, without even realizing what he was doing. With that crazed look in his eye, anything was possible. Rodakis instinctively brought his hands up to his face to protect his head from any possible blows, but Paschalis clamped his wrists tightly in the crook of his arm, pulling them slowly up and leaving his face exposed. He had never suspected that the young man was so strong, so much stronger than he was. Then he felt himself sinking under the sound of the pummelling of the assailant's free fist, which was hitting him much harder than the other one had – but it was more the noise flooding his head than the pain itself, which ruptured all connection with reality. He processed the punches and the pain they inflicted more on an intellectual than a physical level, analyzing them in terms of a logical sequence: He's hitting me, therefore I am in pain. He did not pass out and could therefore see Paschalis climbing off him, getting to his feet and walking away.

The truth is that Paschalis had no intention of pushing him to the ground. Had Rodakis not lost his balance and fallen, it is unlikely that any of what followed would have happened. His fall took things beyond the realm of reason. It signalled the passage across a fine line into the field of battle. From that moment, there was no turning back and a clash was inevitable. Straddling the older man's stomach, he saw a terrified pair of eyes looking up at him, and took this as confirmation that he was in the right. And when Rodakis pulled his hands up over his face to shield himself, Paschalis got even more fired up, taking this as a signal to start pummelling him. The only thing that struck him at that moment was how weak his boss was, cowering behind his arms. He was expecting a little more resistance. And then, with the first punch he administered, he lost all control and abandoned himself to the sweetness of revenge, albeit physical. When it was all over, he rose to his feet and, without the faintest scruple or concern for the injuries he might have inflicted, got up and walked away.

Rodakis was soon on his feet again. The first thing he did was inspect all the bones in his head with his fingers, checking that nothing was broken. Nothing was. He was reassured. Strangely, nothing, not even his lips or his nose, was bleeding. The only thing was a deep cut to the flesh on the inside of his cheek, which he felt with his tongue, which had obviously resulted from a violent collision with his teeth. It would soon pass. The echo of the rapid-fire blows still rang in his head and caused him an agonizing dizziness. Brushing himself down, his first thought was, 'Well, at least that's taken care of.'

Much as Rodakis liked to think that his new enterprise required serious application and research, and much as he liked the idea of setting up a project that might one day lead to a discovery, he was not doing any research at all. He was responsible neither for the original idea nor the subsequent course of events; the whole thing was really Vaya's concern and relied on her instincts rather than his management. All he had to do was attend to the everyday duties of the average bee-keeper, which meant that the bulk of his work was restricted to the summer months.

There was no urgency for him to give up his current job beyond his conviction that if he dedicated himself exclusively to this project, he would increase his chances of success. But there was another reason why he was anxious to leave it; he needed time for Rosa. He firmly believed that her education would benefit more from his tuition than from what the local school had to offer.

Lessons started in the autumn of the same year as the honey project. One of the upstairs rooms was designated as the schoolroom. At first Rodakis intended to use the big room because it was light and the two tall bookcases facing each other created an atmosphere conducive to learning and study. However, since Vaya's bedroom led off it, and her only access to the rest of the house was through the big room, he abandoned that idea because it would mean that Vaya would either be permanently banned from entering her bedroom or permanently locked up inside it during lesson time. Then he thought that from a psychological perspective it would be better if the schoolroom were used exclusively for lessons – a special room that Rosa would consciously have to make her way to, even if it was only a matter of climbing a flight of stairs between the floors of the same house.

The light in the upstairs room was satisfactory. He pushed a shiny dark old wooden table into the middle of the room. He had put up a small blackboard on the wall facing the window, to catch the light, with maps to the left and to the right of it: one of the country, the other of the island. Despite the fact that Rodakis intended to organize a systematic teaching programme for Rosa, in the end it proved impossible to stick to a proper timetable.

Every day at dawn, Rodakis got out of bed to attend to a few small tasks and then shut himself away in the schoolroom for a short time. After a few minutes, he would ring the small bell (the one used in the summer for the honey stall) to let Rosa know that she should make her way upstairs immediately as he was ready to begin. However, the bell never rang at the same time; it always depended both on whether he had finished everything he had to do, and on his mood. But Rosa was expected to be ready. At the beginning of the lesson she would sit on the chair next to his, but after a while would get down, put her hands on his thighs and try to climb up. He cautioned her sternly: 'That is forbidden,' and returned her back to her seat. However, as soon as he did so, Rosa would refuse to pay attention and spent the remainder of the lesson staring out of the window, either chewing the ends of her hair, or scratching the table with her fingernails. Rodakis had to cave in and let her sit on his knee. He told himself that she was still very young, younger than most children starting school. He also noticed that her ability to absorb information as well as her powers of concentration were better on his lap than on her chair. This observation was recorded in the blue book designated for this purpose, along with a wealth of other such observations relating to Rosa's receptiveness to information. It was always on the table next to him.

Rosa slowly succeeded in imposing her will, and the chair soon became a thing of the past. On entering the room, she would give a little skip and fly into his arms. He was not happy about this, and made his feelings clear to her, telling her that she was spoiled and should not be indulged in this way. Nevertheless, he liked having her sit on him and would observe with satisfaction her weight increasing with the passing months, and her legs, stuck fast to his, growing longer, inching their way closer and closer to the floor.

Learning came easily to Rosa. Rodakis quickly concluded that she was an intelligent child, but there were certain things that she closed her mind to and would not take in. For example, although she raced through the alphabet, she would confuse the order of some of the consonants – especially the ones that followed on from each other or sounded very similar. He would repeat the correct order to her, but to no avail. In the end (in this too) rather than convincing Rosa of the importance of the sequence, he only succeeded in convincing himself that it was of no real importance anyway, seeing that she could recognize and sound all the letters; her error was purely formal. He was struck by how serious and intelligent some of her questions were, and how inane others were. It fascinated him and he wondered whether this combination of intelligence and stupidity was nothing more than a symptom of her tender age, or something that would stay with her for life.

It quickly became apparent that Rodakis was not intending to follow a conventional school syllabus. The bias was at the cost of grammar and religious studies, as he had decided that history, mythology, and arithmetic were infinitely more important. Over the next few years anthropology and physics appeared on the curriculum, and he was thrilled that he had the power to deliver even just one child from what he judged to be the useless and inadequate education on offer at the local school. But more than that, he delighted in the chance he had to occupy himself with something as fascinating as moulding a pliable soul and a virgin spirit.

These lessons, just like the experiment, continued uninterrupted for a number of years.

Rodakis recalled how his father never tasted the first honey of the year until it had stayed shut tight inside a jar for at least seventy-two hours. He insisted that it was essential for the flavour to mature and for the aroma to diffuse properly inside the honey. He had a special long-handled silver spoon he used for the first tasting, on the grounds that a noble metal would not corrupt the taste. This was dismissed as one of his eccentricities, and nobody thought that he actually believed it, but with time, the ritual had developed into something of a superstition, and had to be observed. Rodakis did not consider himself to be a superstitious man, but when he decided to go into the honey business himself, he remained true to the tradition of the three-day-wait and the silver spoon, reasoning that his father, had he ever seen the experiment to its conclusion, would have been very punctilious on these two points. For Rodakis, it was something of a tribute to the memory of the man who had inspired the experiment.

Vaya for her part respected the wishes of father and son. In fact, it was Vaya who had reminded Rodakis of the sequence he should follow: as soon as he showed signs of wanting to cut corners in his impatience to taste the new honey, she reined him in, cautioning him sternly that it was not enough for him to lecture Rosa on the importance of self-discipline; he should apply it to himself as well.

When the first honey was ready, Vaya promptly announced that there was great scope for improvement, and a few changes to the proportions in the plants in the enclosure were necessary. She thought that even if this was not true, it would secure another year's safe haven for herself and her daughter.

The second year, after the proportions had been adjusted, there was more at stake. It was more important than the first year because this was the moment of truth, when it would be clear whether there was anything to S. Rodakis's theory or not, and whether adjusting the proportions of the plants had any impact on the quality of the honey. Vaya, aware of what was at stake, spent the three-day period in a state of intense anxiety. Most of the time she was either in a semi-intoxicated condition or occupying herself with meaningless tasks.

When tasting time came, they were both in such a state that it was impossible for them to judge whether or not there was any improvement on the previous year.

'I'm not sure,' said Rodakis, 'I can't tell. What do you think?'

'I don't know. I think it's different. Maybe a bit better.'

Later on Vaya went back down to the cellar where they kept the honey pots, this time taking some of last year's honey with her. She compared the two flavours by nibbling on little pieces of bread in between spoonfuls so she could confidently differentiate between them. She tried to be as calm and objective as possible, and this time saw that there was a difference, that this year's batch really was better, and, moreover, that the improvement was in the direction that she had tried to achieve by tweaking the proportions so that the dry ingredients would dominate over the sweet and the bitter. Without discounting the possibility that it was a mere coincidence, this was undoubtedly a positive sign.

The customers' verdict was unanimous. They kept coming back for more, and back again. Even if three times the quantity of honey had been produced, there still would not have been enough to keep up with demand. Because they were so busy, Vaya had to end her strict policy of isolation and go out front to help serve the customers. That was the summer that E. Rodakis found out about Vaya's existence, when without quite understanding how, she asked her brother if she could borrow his botany book. Shortly after that, Rodakis was to receive the devastating news that his book had been devoured by a dog.

After what Rodakis referred to as the miracle of the second year, he was torn between pushing for further improvements and abandoning the experiment to settle on this combination of plants, known to produce very high quality honey. Vaya's opinion was emphatic and echoed loud and clear through the dining room.

'There is obviously room for improvement. You can be sure of that. It is worth the effort, absolutely worth it.'

In the face of this unshakable certainty, Rodakis was forced to give his consent for the experiment to carry over into a third year. The adjustments were once more left to her, because of her talents for negotiating her way through the maze of flavours. The only thing that mattered to her was that she had succeeded in extending the contract for at least another year. On the other hand, she was aware that her credibility would be called into question, so she would have to do her utmost to achieve some degree, however small, of the improvements she promised. It was not going to be easy. Beyond the rather abstract and dubious nature of the enterprise itself, there was nothing obviously wrong to remedy. That was the problem. Things would have been a lot simpler if there were. As things stood, she had to make something that was already very good even better. While Rodakis and Rosa sat locked away in the schoolroom, she would close her eyes, and spoon in mouth, wait for the honey to slowly melt, trying to reconstruct the elements of the flavour and reconstitute them in new combinations.

Vaya was vindicated for a third year in a row. Her confidence soared. This time the superiority of the honey was so obvious that it was not even necessary to taste it; the two bee-keepers could tell from the aroma that filled the room as soon the undulating mass started to flow into the storage jars. That was enough for them to understand that yet another successful stage had been completed.

That year also saw the arrival of customers from other places. Rising demand prompted them to introduce an advance order system so their customers could be assured of their share before the honey had even been harvested. However, this system only proved efficient the first time it was tried; after that, in the fourth year, as soon as people heard about it, they rushed over to place their orders almost a year in advance. According to many, this led to unequal treatment and ultimately to another dead-end. Moreover, everyone wanted to ensure that they would get at least one jar from the first harvest, because – and no one really understood why – that was the best honey of the lot. No one, that is, except Vaya and Rodakis: Only at the beginning of the production season, and for a lamentably short time, was everything in bloom, so perfect proportions were only obtainable at this time. An unavoidable disadvantage, but it did not detract from the essence of the experiment.

In the fourth and the fifth years, especially in the fifth, there were a few more positive developments, which, although they may not have been obvious to their customers, were nevertheless important from the perspective of the integrity of the experiment. Vaya was manipulating the results and making combinations with the ease of a painter mixing colours on a palette. In everybody's minds, Vaya was inextricably connected with this special honey, especially since she had appeared almost at the same time as it had. Although nobody knew about the experiments and formulas, everyone believed that she was behind Rodakis's phenomenal success, no matter if they could not quite see how.

The disappointing result of the sixth year was not Vaya's fault. Incessant heavy rain and, what was worse, hailstones, which almost completely wiped out the more vulnerable of the plants, put paid to all their plans for that year. Customers, drawn by the reputation of the honey, made a special journey to the island to procure a small amount. After going to such lengths to get their hands on some, they were very disappointed. Sitting in the harbour coffee houses, they would complain to anybody who would listen that they were the victims of exaggerated rumours and had wasted a lot of money and made the long journey for nothing. Attempts to explain that this was a bad year and that the honey more than merited its reputation, were met with scepticism.

Those who gave the honey a second chance were handsomely compensated. The seventh year turned out to be the best year of all, so good that Rodakis told Vaya to stop experimenting because they were going to settle on this as the final formula. The proportions of sweet, dry and bitter were perfect. Vaya protested.

'Don't you think I should have some say in this decision?' she shouted, hurling the floor cloth onto the tiles in a fit of fury.

Rodakis was astonished. In all the years they had been living together, neither he nor she had ever broken decorum with displays of extreme disaffection – or satisfaction. Vaya insisted that they could not stop now – however thrilled he was with the result. She argued that it would amount to a betrayal of the experiment if they stopped before they had established that there was absolutely no more room for improvement. Once again, Rodakis reluctantly gave in, but he could not shake off the image he now had of Vaya looking like a compulsive card player, who, incapable of walking away from the table to enjoy his winnings, clings to the anxiety of risk.

The eighth year gave the lie both to Vaya's promises and her expectations; nobody argued that the honey was of a rare aroma, but it was clearly inferior to that of the previous year. Rodakis felt vindicated in his insistence that they stop while they were ahead, but did not say as much because he didn't want to be accused of gloating. He waited for Vaya to acknowledge her mistake and abandon the experiment – however belatedly.

But Vaya did nothing of the kind. Instead, she started to talk with great enthusiasm about some divine inspiration she had had that would bring renewed impetus to the experiment. Rodakis put his foot down. He refused to listen, rejecting any possibility of prolonging the experiment, which, he told her, no longer held the same fascination for him that it once had; he was looking to turn his attention to other fields and occupy himself in new areas. He would keep the bees on as a source of income, that was that, selling the honey produced from the formula from the seventh year at a big profit.

'They won't take up any of your time,' she said, clearly desperate,

'I'll see to everything, even the plants. You won't have to do a thing, you can devote yourself to your new interests. Just let me keep it going, that's all I ask.'

After a short time she added:

'Unless we've become too much for you, Rosa and I; if that's the case we'll pack, and leave right away.'

Rodakis looked her straight in the eye and with a very grave expression on his face said:

'I have made a commitment to Rosa. I have assumed the responsibility for her education. If that's what you're worried about, that I intend to kick her out of this house – and I believe that that is exactly what you are worried about, and have been for some time – let me assure you, I have no such intentions. You are both free to stay here in this house, as you have been doing all these years, for as long as you wish.'

After that, Vaya felt that she had neutralized her most oppressive fear. Two things were clear: first, her continued presence at the house had little to do with the experiment and everything to do with Rosa. This was so obvious: she marvelled at how she had failed to see it before. The second point was that as the years went by, the so-called experiment was no longer just a means to secure her position in the house; it had started to take on special meaning for her. With the threat of homelessness gone, she saw how passionately she wanted to defend the project, and she was willing to fight for its survival, if only for one more year.

She felt it wise not to broach the subject immediately. A few days went by and one evening, as the three of them were sitting at the dinner table, she went straight to the heart of the matter:

'What a pity you don't want us to make one last attempt.'

Rodakis understood at once what she was referring to and tried to sound as indifferent as possible:

'Yes, I remember that new inspiration you had – how you wanted to try again. But you never elaborated.'

She saw through this show of indifference right away; after all these years, she had learned how to read him, and realized that all this time he'd been dying to hear what she was thinking, but his pride kept him from asking.

'Didn't elaborate? If you remember, it was you who cut me short. We nearly came to blows over it. It's a pity. A real pity.'

'It can't do any harm to hear it. But my decision to stop the experiment stands. Let's hear it – what was this moment of insight?'

'Exactly that, a moment of insight: It dawned on me that what we needed was something new: reworking the same combinations over and over again was pointless, like you said. Then I thought of the heather that grows back home, the one with the white flowers and a scent you don't find anywhere else, not on any flower. If we could get hold of some, we could be producing honey so divine that even the gods on Olympus would queue up to buy it.'

'That's it? Your moment of insight? Adding a new plant?' he asked, visibly disappointed.

'It might not seem like much to you; but if you could trust me a little – just this once…'

'A plant we can't even get hold of!'

'The mountains back home are full of it. In the evening when the breeze is up, their scent wafts all the way down to the sea. Of course I couldn't go back. You could make the journey – if you wanted to. But you don't.'

'I made that clear from the beginning.'

They wished each other a good night and retired to their respective bedrooms. A little later Vaya heard footsteps outside her door. She got out of bed and saw a piece of paper shining on the floor. It was a note:

'I've given the matter some more thought. I've reconsidered. I'll be waiting for you at dawn in the kitchen for directions. I'll set off in the morning and try to be back the day after. Hope you're satisfied.'

Whenever the wind was up, a rhythmic banging noise could be heard from the upper floor. The noise was not very loud, but was extremely insistent, like a constant reminder of some unfinished business. A plank of wood from the overhang above the schoolroom window had come loose and would swing back and forth in the wind, making that banging noise. This had been going on for some time.

Vaya was the only one who appeared to be bothered by it. She had repeatedly asked Rodakis to attend to it, but all he did was knock the odd nail into it, which provided only temporary relief because much of the plank was rotten and the incessant assault from his nails only weakened it further. He did not seem to mind it, not even during lesson time. Neither did Rosa; but then, not even the mightiest of explosions could break her concentration.

'I can't believe it didn't disturb you,'Vaya said to her one day.

'What didn't?'

'That plank, banging non-stop like that during the lesson.'

'I didn't hear anything.'

Her apathy infuriated Vaya. 'Well, since I'm the only one that wretched thing is bothering,' she said to herself, 'I'll just have it deal with it myself.'

Her nerves were already somewhat frayed as this had coincided with the three-day wait and judgement on her determination to introduce a new plant to the formula would soon be passed. That incessant banging was the last thing she needed. She marched up to the schoolroom, determined to remove the rotten piece of wood once and for all, as all attempts to repair it had been futile; then Rodakis would be forced to replace it.

'Who would have thought,' she muttered as she tried to dislodge it, 'that he used to do this sort of thing for a living? Now he can't even be bothered to replace a piece of rotten wood.'

The offending plank offered minimal resistance, and Vaya let it fall into the garden with a sense of satisfaction. She allowed her gaze to rest on the open horizon; the atmosphere had been swept clear by the winds, so much so that she could make out even the most distant houses, the ones built above the harbour several kilometres away. Clear days like this were unusual for the time of year.

The view from the upstairs windows was her only contact with the outside world. In all the years she had lived there, she never once left the property. Communication with other people was limited to the few words she exchanged with their customers during the summer, always kept to the absolute minimum needed to complete the transactions. At first Rodakis put this down to the fears of a persecuted woman, but as time went on, he suspected that deep down she wanted a quiet life away from other people, just as he did.

Her eyes scaled the houses that were visible in the distance; in the sunlight some of them stood out in relief; others looked more blurred, as if they were starting to evaporate. For the first time, feelings of curiosity welled up inside her; curiosity about the people who lived in those houses, coupled with a new desire to go to those strange places and walk down the street with other people again, to see the sea close up, to see images other than those framed by her windows (which by now were safely stored away in her memory down to their every last detail, in the same way that she used to store visual information about the hidden landscapes inside Rodakis's cupboards and drawers).

Rodakis was out buying supplies. Rosa normally went with him but had stayed at home that day. Dumbfounded, she watched Vaya wind a scarf around her head, explaining that she was going out and that Rosa had better behave herself while she was away. She could not remember her mother ever leaving the house before. She hadn't given it any thought either, until now, when it was actually happening, and the whole idea struck her as unnatural and unreal.

'Your father will be back soon. So will I.'

Making her way out of the house, it suddenly occurred to Vaya that she had lost the habit of walking as she had been moving around such a confined space for so many years. Her gait was uncertain, and gave her the false impression that the ground was strewn with invisible traps. She took a deep, anxious breath; the air was cool and invigorating, and gave her the courage she needed for the reckless act of leaving the property. Her heart was racing, even though she knew that the nearest houses were some distance away.

She paused at the big tree she could see from her bedroom window, alone and erect among the bushes. Rodakis had explained to her that the tree was the dowry of some girl who had never married. (It was customary on the island for fathers to plant 'dowry trees' when their daughters were born. When the time came for a girl to get married, her father would cut down the tree, sell it as firewood, and put the money towards her dowry.) She scrutinized the cracks in the bark and the variations in the colour of the trunk, details her eagle-sharp vision could not appreciate from the distance of her window. She wondered what had held her back all these years, what had kept her within the four walls, never daring to venture outside even for a short walk around the nearby isolated areas. The fissured bark of the dark tree trunk held no answers.

She walked on. Her legs were gradually growing accustomed to the ground, and her pulse had started to settle. She did not take the road to the burned forest. There were half-withered bushes all around her; the mountain stood to her right; ahead of her lay the houses she could see from her window, although just then they were obscured by the hilltops. She kept walking, following the same line her eye had travelled along earlier as she stood gazing out of the schoolroom window.

A short distance outside the village, by one of the island's four harbours, stood an abandoned chapel. Vaya stopped and leant against its convex wall. The village proper was a bit further down, and she had to make up her mind whether to turn back or let herself be swept along by this unprecedented impulsiveness and walk among strangers once more in a world she had been exiled from for so long.

The die was cast. And after a while her steps brought her to the first house of the village, or, depending on the direction you were coming from, the last. It was an old, prosperous-looking house with a mauve flowering plant climbing up its weathered walls. She peered cautiously in through an open window. The sun was sinking, but there was more than enough light for her to make out the three people inside.

A man and a woman sat opposite each other at a narrow table, playing cards. Watching the game behind them was an old woman confined to a wheelchair by some disability. The couple played on in silence, without expression, while the old woman's face betrayed a lively interest, despite the fact that she could not get a very good view from where she was sitting. At some point the man rose to his feet and gave the woman a hard slap. She received the assault without protest, although the agony was written across her face. The man sat down again and the game resumed. A few cards were played and then it was the woman's turn to stand up. She grabbed hold of the birch twigs leaning against the chair next to her; one single but violent stroke was enough to catch her husband on the hand. He rubbed the painful spot with his other hand. She sat down and dealt. Every now and then one of the two would stand up (from what she could see, it depended on who was winning) and having inflicted a wound on their opponent, would get on with the game. Vaya observed that the exposed areas of flesh on both players were covered in bruises, weals and swellings. Whenever the man stood up ready to strike, the cripple got very agitated and would bang her fist on the armrest of her wheelchair, open her mouth as if to scream, but couldn't and had to content herself with thumping her wheelchair. However, when it was the woman's turn to attack, the old woman's face radiated profound satisfaction and joy. All of this was played out under the innocent gaze of an elderly man smiling down on them from a portrait on the wall facing them.

Vaya was mesmerized by this bizarre spectacle, and stood there watching covertly for quite some time. She would have lingered even longer had the old woman not suddenly raised her finger and pointed to the window where Vaya stood, trying with muffled noises to alert the couple to the presence of the voyeur. They just ignored her and carried on with their game, but Vaya, terrified by the thought that she had been seen, promptly fled.

A little further along was a small cluster of buildings. They were not houses but Vaya could not tell whether they were used as shops or warehouses. One of them, instead of shutters had thick iron bars, suggesting that the owner stored things of value inside, but in fact the building was full of onions and garlic, either hanging in plaits from the wall or piled up on the floor. There was a monkey in there too, tied to a rusty old iron ring screwed into the wall. As soon as it noticed Vaya, it started performing somersaults and leapt up and down in a frenzy of delight before grabbing a few onions, juggling with them and pulling faces at the same time.

'Good Lord!' she whispered. 'Whatever next!'

Apart from the two bizarre spectacles greeting her at the entrance to the village, everything else looked absolutely normal. The houses were clean and well maintained, and everybody seemed to be going about their daily business. Her fear of being among people again almost evaporated when she saw that nobody was taking any notice of her. They looked at her and instantly looked away, totally indifferent, which made her wonder how it was possible for an intruder to attract so little attention in a small community such as this.

She walked down to the harbour; not the harbour where she'd left the boat (or rather where the boat had left her) when she first arrived on the island. That one, as far as she could tell, was the main port, whereas this was nothing more than a large inlet where a few boats, mostly fishing boats, were anchored. Whenever she stopped and took stock of how far she had come, she felt like running back. But then it occurred to her that what she was doing was the most natural thing in the world, and she remonstrated with herself for waiting so long to do it. Her spirit vacillated between those two extremes. She walked the length of the harbour back and forth three times.

The third time, she noticed a coffee house on the ground floor of a two-storey house. It had shabby, nondescript curtains and a sign suspended awkwardly above the door saying *The Good Soul*. A tremor shot through her as she read those words: this phrase was usually used of people on their deathbeds, or at any rate people who only had death to look forward to. At that moment she felt as if the message was intended for her, but then she thought that it was probably just a variation on the very common *The Kind Heart*, and this reassured her.

She went up to the door and had a look inside. The coffee house was full, with one free table, two at a pinch. She desperately wanted to go in, sit down and order a nice cup of coffee. But she could never go and sit down with all those people in there. On the other hand, the fact that there were so many people meant that it would be easier for her to walk in without drawing attention, just go in and disappear into the crowd.

She opened the door and looked inside to see if there was a table somewhere she could sit. Nobody turned to look at her, which made her happy. Every person on every single table was caught up in animated discussions about different subjects no doubt, but with the same passion and intensity: expressed in raised voices, rolling eyes, reddened cheeks; in conspiratorial whispers and dark looks. Nobody was gambling which was unusual for a coffee house. Everybody was engaged in conversation. Yes, there were two free tables, and one at the back, out of the way. But when she made to sit down at it, she saw that it was already taken because somebody had left their things on it: a small chemist's bottle and some embroidery. The other table was right in the middle of the room. She didn't like that; she didn't like the idea of being looked at from all angles. However, the continuing indifference to her presence subdued her fears and she eventually sat down.

Almost immediately, a woman appeared from the back of the room and sat down at the table with the medicine and the embroidery. As soon as she spotted the new arrival, she jumped up and approached with hurried little steps.

'What can I get you?'

Vaya ordered a cup of unsweetened coffee. Watching the woman move off, she wondered if she was the 'good soul' of the sign outside. While she was waiting for her coffee, she lifted the hem of her skirt, unpicked a few stitches and removed a couple of coins from its folds. Vaya had sewn money into all her clothes, money she had saved up on the sly from the income from the honey every summer, to have it at hand in case of an emergency, if she was ever unfortunate enough to find herself homeless and penniless again.

Four other tables, with very little space between them, surrounded Vaya's table. Behind them were dozens more which, arranged in geometrical patterns, imposed a sense of order on the crowded room. After she finished her coffee, she started to relax a little. Everybody was oblivious to her anyway and she noticed that this indifference was not, as she had initially supposed, restricted to her; there was absolutely no communication across tables. Each group was independent; it was as if they did not even know each other. They were all caught up in their own discussions – more in keeping with an assembly hall in a big city than a rural coffee house.

The only woman there besides herself and the proprietor, from what she could see, was sitting at the table directly in front of her with two men. At the table to her right were two more men. One was eating and the other was drinking wine. The drinker was

clutching a handkerchief, and every now and then would use it to wipe the tears from his eyes. The sight of a man crying in public made an impression on Vaya and she started trying to listen in on their conversation, isolating it as much as she could from the general hum of the room.

'You'll get used to it,' said the chewer, his mouth full. 'It'll be hard at first. Coming home to an empty house. But you'll get used to it.'

'It'll be an even bigger change for her,' said the drinker, wiping his eyes again.

'Hmm.'

'It will.'

His companion, still chewing, said something Vaya didn't catch. The drinker probably didn't hear it either. It was only what he said after he had finished swallowing that was comprehensible.

' – just like I got used to mine. I used to think I could see her, standing there in front of me – awake, not dreaming. But now, a lot of time has passed, and I wonder whether I wasn't dreaming after all, and just thought I was awake. Then I just stopped seeing her – awake or dreaming.'

'That's a shame.'

'No. It's much better this way. The living with the living and the…'

'Do you think I'll be able to see her too? Mine?' came the question, with just a glimmer of hope in his voice.

'It doesn't happen to everybody, you know. Much better for you if you don't.'

'…and the dead with the dead.'

'Now you're talking.'

There was a hiatus in the conversation: the one busy with his plate, the other with his glass.

Vaya then turned her attention to the table to her left. The three men sitting there were speaking in low, not exactly conspiratorial voices, but in a way that made you suspect they were discussing something very important. However hard she strained, she couldn't understand what they were talking about. The only thing that was clear was that one of them was arguing a point that one of the others disagreed with, while the third member of the party looked at each of them in turn, rolling his eyes as he did so. It was not until much later that something representative of the debate was said. It was spoken by the sceptic:

'Whatever you say, there's no way you'll ever convince me that there are still lions on this island.'

So that was the issue: the man had been trying to convince his friends that lions still roamed the island. He even argued that there had always been lions on the island, going right back to antiquity when the inhabitants fashioned idols of all shapes and sizes and farmers were still ploughing them up, even today. They'd been told to turn them in to the president of the council if they found any.

'And what do these lions live on? Pigeons, I suppose?'

'Animals. Like the ones we hunt.'

'So how come we never see them?'

'Lots of people have. My late brother for one; then there's the baker's sister, you know, the one who lost her mind.'

'Oh, I see. Dead men and madmen.'

'What about the captain's niece? Which is she – dead or mad?'

'Mad? Mad? She's a raving lunatic – claims she turns into a cat at night and goes climbing trees!'

Vaya followed all this in bewilderment, not knowing which of the two she found more convincing. The man sitting in the crossfire rolling his eyes probably had the same problem. She felt a shudder of fear and wondered whether it was wise to go walking around like she had, along that deserted stretch, alone and unprotected – but one thing was certain: she hadn't seen any lions on her way.

'There are lions here. And sooner or later, everyone will have proof.'

'Let's see the proof first.'

The debate continued with new arguments on both sides, but in even lower voices. Vaya was straining to hear what they were saying, her posture betraying her curiosity: she was leaning over so far in the direction of their table that her body tilted at an unnatural angle, and her neck craned to such an extent that it looked like her head had sprouted an enormous ear. She came to with a start when she noticed that the rolling eyes had abandoned their back-and-forth loop between his companions and had settled on her. She immediately pretended that she wasn't listening, raised her water glass, and drank half of it with an innocent look on her face, convincing enough for the rolling eyes to resume their former rhythm.

'It's too soon,' said the chewer from the first table. 'Wait for the forty days 'til the memorial service. Do her forty days for her and take it from there. And you'll see – it'll still be too soon. Wait 'til after the three-month memorial. Take it from there.'

'Three months is a long time,' replied the drinker.

'Don't make any hasty decisions. Do her three months for her and then decide. If you still want to leave the island after that, well…'

Then something happened that made everybody at the surrounding tables look up. The woman sitting with the two men at the table in front of Vaya's suddenly shot to her feet in a fit of outrage. One of the two men pulled her by the wrist back down into her chair and said in a conciliatory voice:

'All right. All right. You can have the painting as well.'

'And the three bronzes,' the woman replied, with great determination.

The two men looked at each other and nodded.

The woman spoke again, calmer this time.

'What about that bedside table?'

Vaya had the impression that they were brothers and a sister, fighting over their inheritance – only they weren't discussing anything of value, like houses or land, just worthless objects, like small children squabbling over their toys, which made the whole scene rather comical. Vaya was struggling not to laugh; she was beginning to enjoy being back among people – a prospect that only a short time ago had terrified her. She found other people's conversations, however banal they might be, fascinating.

'Don't forget the village constable.' A raised voice from the table to her left was heard for the first time.

'Oh no! Here we go again.'

'The constable – you mean the one who got savaged by jackals?' asked the man in the middle tentatively.

'The one they found eaten alive, that's right. But was it really a jackal that got him? Everyone who saw the body, what was left of it, I mean, said that teeth marks like that, well...'

'Oh please!'

'What about the tooth marks, what do you mean?'

'Only a large carnivore can leave tooth marks that size.'

The man in the middle sank his rolling eyes in his hands. The others stopped talking for a moment.

'The tiled stove – as well as the lamp? No. I can't have that. You'll have to make a choice one or the other,' said the one man to the other.

'You'll have to choose,' echoed the woman.

The other man looked at them, deep in thought.

'The first time I met her,' the drinker had come to life again, 'I thought she was really ugly. I remember thinking, "There's no way I'm marrying her." But then her hands started looking better, her eyes prettier, her mouth and her ears too. In the end, I said to myself, "You're a lucky man, getting set up with such a good match." The day before yesterday I saw her lying on the bed, dead, and I stood there thinking that the prettiest girl on the island had died. Yesterday I packed up all her things, her clothes, everything. After that, I don't know how it happened; I saw one of her hairs, caught under a chair leg. I'd been through all her things; none of it had bothered me, none of it. But when I saw that hair…when I saw her hair…'

He slammed his face his handkerchief against his face, letting the tears flow noiselessly. His companion, who'd finished eating, for want of anything useful to say, not knowing what to say, started wiping his bowl clean with a piece of bread.

All of a sudden, silence descended on the three tables. The buzz of conversation continued elsewhere in the coffee house. This was a short, local silence, a black hole in the middle of the noisy room. At the table to Vaya's left, each of the three friends, having reached a stalemate regarding the proof of the existence of lions, started looking round in different directions. At the table in front, the siblings were lost in their own private thoughts concerning the compromise that would be most advantageous to them, and at the table to the right, the muted weeping went on unabated.

Then, as if in response to some invisible signal, the three tables simultaneously resumed their respective conversations. Although Vaya had finished her coffee, she lingered at her table, gathering snippets from various conversations, by now totally abstracted from her own reality. But she was jolted back to it by something said by the woman at the table in front. She and her brothers had completed the process of dividing their inheritance and were now allowing themselves to discuss all and sundry.

'I'm getting up early tomorrow to knead some honey bread.'

This statement cut through Vaya, reminding her of her new honey lying tightly sealed inside the ceramic jars, waiting to be tasted the next day. It quickly dawned on her that she had been away for hours; she wondered what Rodakis would think when he realized that she had gone off like that, without warning. Rosa might be worried. It looked like it was going to rain and, tempted though she was to order a second cup of coffee, she had to get going. She stood up, crossed the room, once more failing to arouse the slightest interest in anyone. Perhaps Rodakis was not the only one who liked to keep himself to himself; the whole island was just as strange. She opened the door and stepped outside. It was drizzling; she didn't mind. It was a warm evening, and she was quite hardy. She set off at a quick pace, hoping to be home before nightfall.

At first light Rodakis went down to see if Vaya was back. All Rosa had been able to tell him was that she had said she wouldn't be long. But he had been up late, and she had failed to return. 'What a peculiar woman,' he thought. He considered it possible that she had been delayed by the two-hour storm that had broken the evening before and might have forced her to spend the night away. However, that did not answer the question of why she had left in the first place, or where she had gone; Rodakis was sure that Vaya would not have left without a very good reason.

He went downstairs and headed towards her bedroom. He opened the door very quietly. Rosa was asleep, alone; Vaya had not been back. He walked over to the bed; she was fast asleep, suggesting that she had stayed awake well into the night waiting for her mother. Her right shoulder was bare, white and rounded. It gave off a faint light. He touched it. She did not stir.

Midday and still no sign of Vaya: Rodakis's irritation was slowly mounting. He was not worried; he was annoyed by the disruption to his routine. Moreover, this was no ordinary day. It was tasting day. Her absence made him even more anxious to see the results of this year's experiment – the last year of experimentation, if he had his way. He wanted to wait for her so they could taste the honey together, like they did every year.

Rosa was clearly distressed, despite her efforts to hide it. She felt a horrible tightening in her stomach, and when lunchtime came, she didn't touch the peas Vaya had cooked shortly before she left. It was only later that afternoon that she was made, or rather forced, to sit down to eat, and listen to Rodakis's stern injunctions and arguments, which did not help matters.

'What if your mother doesn't come back?' he kept asking her.

'Will that mean that you're never going to eat again?' She did not answer.

The same argument applied to his own situation: if Vaya never came back, would the honey remain sealed in the jars, forever unsampled? This line of reasoning enabled him to overcome his hesitation and he decided to go ahead alone. It was hardly his fault – Vaya was unforgivably late.

That was when that the episode involving the silver spoon took place: the spoon was needed for the tasting, and he had to empty two drawers out onto the kitchen floor before he found it stuffed inside the pocket of the old silk dressing gown. This unfortunate incident added tension to an already charged atmosphere.

The cellar was drenched in semi-darkness, but he did not need much light. What he did need was the tasting spoon, and that, thankfully, had been found. Rodakis stood in front of the three storage jars holding the first harvest of the year. With controlled movements, he removed the lid from one of the jars and plunged the spoon into it.

The moment he closed his lips round the laden spoon, the honey exploded inside his mouth; he felt like he was under attack from some overwhelming force, striking him like a thunderbolt and leaving him dazed inside a cloud of mist. From within this mist, emerged a mischievous little cherub, which started fluttering around the ceiling, from corner to corner, while the opening bars of a triumphant march were heard in the distance. It did not take long for the aroma from the opened jar to pervade the entire room, like gas suddenly escaping from a cylinder. Its presence was so manifest that Rodakis thought that it was actually visible, that it that was the mist cloud enshrouding him.

Convinced from the first that he was having another hallucination, he kept his eyes and his ears wide open, not wanting the slightest detail of this unreal, divine apparition to escape him,

before it faded and evaporated. He was right. The mist collapsed, swallowing up the frisky little angel as it did so, and the exuberant fanfare made way for the screech of Rosa's chair leg as it scraped the tiled floor overhead. He sat down on the floor, clutching the open storage jar tightly in his embrace.

Everything had reverted to its customary dimensions. This had not happened to him for a long time. Silently forming the words with his lips, he asked, 'Why is this happening? Why now?'

He knew the answer. He knew that ever since he stopped being a child, each incidence of this phenomenon, every hallucination, was related to a profound psychological event. Only the honey could have done this. He inverted the silver spoon and sank it back into the jar.

It wasn't simply the best honey he had ever tasted – there was no question about that; somehow, he could feel the taste acting directly on his mood. There were no angels this time, no trumpets. Instead he was flooded with emotion and an unexpected eruption of old sensations, the kind that last only a few seconds in a dream, and are difficult to describe and even harder to recall, the kind that can only be relived by chance in some other dream. There was definitely more to it than a pleasing taste and a potent aroma. He needed a second opinion and Vaya's absence weighed down on him again. But there was always Rosa.

He carried the jar upstairs, eager to see her reaction. Nearing the top of the staircase, he heard voices. 'At last. She's back,' he said to himself and went inside, expecting to see Vaya. Instead, to his surprise, he found Rosa chatting away to the priest and the president of the village council. Seeing the pair of them standing there, he automatically recalled the day they came up to the house to broker the subject of Vaya's guardianship.

'Ah! Here's your father,' said the president.

'Run along now and read your book, there's a good girl.' The priest's tone left no room for negotiation.

'What book?' she asked, genuinely puzzled.

'Go and choose one.'

'Off you go,' said Rodakis, abruptly, at which Rosa immediately turned tail and left.

'Can we go in here?' asked the president.

Rodakis showed them into the big room, just as he had on their first visit.

'I'm afraid this is not a social call,' muttered the priest.

'What's going on?'

'Vaya not here?'

'No. She's been gone since yesterday. It's very strange.'

Priest and president exchanged glances.

'There was something wrong with her foot, wasn't there?' asked the president, and with a sly look added:

'I mean, you'd know if there was, wouldn't you?'

'The toes of one foot are severed.'

'She's dead,' said the priest.

Speechless, Rodakis placed the honey jar on top of the table.

'Last night in the storm. Struck by lightning, poor thing. Some shepherds found her this morning, and came to find the president. She was under a tree.'

'I wasn't completely sure it was her,' said the president, 'but what you said about her toes being – '

'Do you want me to break it to the little one?' asked Father Chryssanthos.

Rodakis shook his head.

'I'll leave that to you then, and I'll take care of everything else. The funeral, and other arrangements. God is great, and his ways inscrutable to men.'

'Yes,' said Rodakis flatly.

'We'll be on our way then; there'll be difficult times ahead.'

The priest left, tailed by the president.

Rodakis washed the silver spoon and dried it carefully. He picked up the jar and climbed the stairs.

'So innocent!' he thought when he saw Rosa in the schoolroom reading a book, exactly as she had been instructed by the priest.

'Have they gone?' she asked as soon as she saw him.

'Yes,' he answered, and she closed her book, judging her obligation to have come to an end. She looked at the jar with curiosity.

Rodakis sat down next to her.

'I'd like you to taste it.'

He filled the spoon and placed it in her mouth. Rosa allowed the thick mass to linger in her mouth for some time. Her face remained expressionless. She raised her fingertips to the edge of her cheek as though trying to use them to help her form a precise opinion.

'Well?' asked Rodakis, taking the rise and fall of her throat as a sign that the honey had at last been swallowed. 'What do you think?'

She looked him straight in the eye, serious.

'This honey is...' she paused. A short interlude. '...fit for angels.'

Rodakis smiled. 'I like that,' he said and leant over and kissed the down under her hairline. And told her that her mother was dead.

The priest was right when he predicted difficult times ahead. That same night was difficult. Rosa eventually fell asleep at daybreak, her grief vanquished by exhaustion. Rodakis went outside and took a solitary walk around his property. Vaya's image kept coming into his head: her face, semi-illuminated by a streak of subdued lamplight, her steady gaze penetrating lance-like, deep into his eyes. But he could not remember when or why she had looked at him with that predatory stare. Then he recalled with emotion the excitement both at the beginning of the experiment and at each step along the way. He thought that it was a pity that she had not lived just one day longer to taste the final triumph of her achievement.

However, Rodakis's distress over Vaya's death was more a concern for Rosa's grief than anything else. Because what filled his heart at that moment, what shone through the darkness of these sad tidings, was an ineffable joy surrounding the discovery he had made a few hours earlier in the cellar. He knew that the wound opened by Vaya's death would inevitably close, but the other thing, the important thing, the treasure stored inside those jars which would fill thousands more, the formula which had produced this treasure would endure. It was immortal, more than immortal: it was powerful. Perhaps it was not completely clear to him what exactly this power consisted of, or what he could do with it, but he did know that he was in possession of a magic key of inestimable worth. Each stride he took in the damp soil was confirmation of the dominance, every breath an infusion of greatness.

With these thoughts in mind, and his gaze fixed firmly ahead at the rising sun, he paced the length of his property. He went from one end to the other, back and over again. And none of the grandeur of this exultation would have been lost, had he not, just moments before reaching the door, felt the earth recede beneath his feet. He had stumbled on a rise, setting clumps of grainy soil spinning everywhere, flying into his eyes, his nose, his ears, and his mouth. He had not fully recovered from the shock of his fall when he saw, caught between his legs, a semi-rotten plank of wood with a couple of nails protruding dangerously from it which had ripped his trousers and torn into his flesh. More instinctively than anything else, he lifted his head and looked up and spotted the gap in the overhang above the upstairs window.

He stood up, spat, dusted himself down, and went inside. Armed with a few nails and a hammer, he climbed the stairs and nailed the rotten plank back into position.

the monastery

As he walked through the entrance to the estate, T. Rosenmann tried to imagine how the baron would react when he saw the gift he had brought him. Later, waiting in the great hall, gazing out through the large windows at the ducks and geese on the artificial lake, the same thought occupied him, and was probably responsible for the smile that had fixed itself on his lips. This was the first thing the baron noticed when he entered the hall.

'My word! You are in good spirits!'

'I always find reasons to be cheerful, Baron, even if I have to invent them,' replied T. Rosenmann, his smile turning to laughter.

'Welcome back. I wasn't expecting you so soon,' remarked the baron, his eyes falling on the large leather-covered box under his visitor's arm.

'Yes. I had intended to stay longer, but was suddenly overcome by the desire to return.'

'Comfortable journey?'

'Tolerable, I dare say; I didn't really notice.'

'Why the hasty departure?'

'No reason. I simply felt like coming home.'

'I won't press the point,' said the baron, directing his gaze once more at the box.

T. Rosenmann, aware of his friend's curiosity, decided to exploit it a little longer and shifted the box to his other arm.

'If you do not wish to divulge the reasons for your premature departure, whatever it was that caused you to alter your plans so suddenly and distracted you so much so that you were not even aware of the circumstances of your journey, so be it. You do not have to explain yourself to me.'

T. Rosenmann laughed like a father indulging his petulant daughter.

'I told you, it was simply the mood I was in. I suddenly found I had no more appetite for the place and felt it was time to leave.'

'Nevertheless, I assume something triggered this mood; and this is something that you wish to keep from me. I reiterate: you do not owe me an explanation.'

'I assume something triggered this mood...' repeated T. Rosenmann in a mock-contemplative tone, and shifted the package once more, back to the original arm. 'Baron – you assume correctly.'

'May I ask why you don't put that package down instead of standing there wearing yourself out?'

'Oh, this!' he said, pretending to have forgotten about its existence. 'It's for you. It's a gift. Don't open it here. Why don't we go and sit outside? It's such a beautiful day.'

The baron motioned towards the French windows. They stepped outside and it was only after they had sat down in the kiosk that T. Rosenmann handed over the box. But when the baron untied the ribbon and tried to open it, an assertive hand falling onto the lid obstructed him.

'Before you open it, Baron: I must confess you were quite right in your insistence that something took place which affected my mood and hastened my return. Having said that, I can assure you it was something of a pleasant nature and is intimately connected with the contents of this box,' he said tapping the lid with his index finger.

'Pleasant?'

'An inadequate description, perhaps. Please, open it.'

The baron hurriedly removed the lid. The box, lined with a shimmering fabric, was empty apart from a minuscule phial of perfume nestling in a depression in its centre.

'Perfume? Thank you so much. I must confess I was unaware that the country you visited was famed for its fine scents.'

T. Rosenmann looked at him with an enigmatic smile.

'So this perfume was responsible for changing your plans?' asked the baron as he extracted the bottle from its niche. 'Let us have a look at the label. Forgive me; this is not a script I am familiar with.'

'It's not perfume.' T. Rosenmann lowered his voice and, deploying all his ventriloquial skills, spoke without moving his lips.

The baron looked confused.

'Did you say something?'

'Baron, this is not perfume,' he said, making full use of his lips this time.

'I don't understand. If it's not perfume, what is it?'

'Honey.'

The baron tried his hardest to conceal his astonishment but was betrayed by the expression in his eyes.

'Honey. Thank you again – you have my word that I shall try to do it justice at breakfast tomorrow. Please don't take offence, but may I ask why you've brought me such a modest quantity? Frankly, this will hardly stretch to two slices of bread.'

T. Rosenmann laughed so loudly that he provoked the geese on the other side of the lake into angry squawks.

'No! I simply cannot allow you to perform such an act of barbarism. Listen to him – spreading it on his bread!'

'I am at a loss to understand anything you say,' declared the baron, clearly offended. 'You're being so cryptic and mysterious. As it happens, I do spread honey on my bread and it has never crossed my mind that to do so was in any way reprehensible.'

'Of course it isn't – and as soon as you hear what I have to say, all these mysteries will be cleared up. Would you care to take a stroll down to the lake?'

'No. I'm in no mood at all to see the ducks, I can assure you. I don't know why; they have become rather aggressive recently. Only the day before yesterday, when I was throwing pieces of bread to them, three of them turned on me. All at once. One of them injured me quite badly, actually.'

'Injured you?'

'Yes. It attacked my leg. Since then I've been wondering whether I should replace the lot of them with goldfish. But go ahead; I'm eager to hear what you have to say.'

T. Rosenmann began to recount the events of his trip.

'When I left for my tour of the islands, the only thing I had in mind was to spend as much time as possible by the sea and enjoy the landscape I'd heard so much about. I thought that if I was lucky, I might be able to bribe one of the locals into securing me an attractive relic from antiquity, part of a temple, or a statue, or some coins. My original intention had been to bring you back something of that nature.'

'I see,' said the baron, brooding over the fact that in place of ancient coins, he now owned a microscopic quantity of honey.

'I didn't stay longer than two days on the first island I visited (its name keeps escaping me; sounds like some kind of spice – that I do know), because I couldn't find any suitable accommodation there. In this respect, I was much more fortunate on the second island. I rented the entire first floor of a ship owner's house for a fortnight. It had uninterrupted views of the sea, rocks and gulls. I would spend the days walking, or would hire a small boat to visit the otherwise inaccessible coastlines and caves the sailor knew like the back of his hand. But the evenings bored me. I had no appetite for reading – it felt too much like being at home. All I did was sit out on my little square balcony, sometimes counting the stars, sometimes the fireflies – apart from the two evenings when the boatman invited me to the waterfront where they'd organised some kind of festivities: grilled fish and traditional music. On both occasions, although over two hundred people were expected, no more than about thirty actually appeared – basically the organisers and their families. I gradually realised that the islanders were not very sociable, and would sooner stay at home than go rushing off to dances. On the second of these evenings, I was approached by a man, a fisherman most probably, who used a hotchpotch of gestures and gesticulations, and a mish-mash of words from various languages, to explain that he wanted to sell me a map at a price agreeable to me. From the general manner with which he handled our negotiations, I understood that this was not the first time he had done this; in fact he approached all foreign visitors to the island as a matter of course.'

'What sort of map was it?'

'A rather poor sketch map showing the way to a remote house. It did occur to me (I don't know why, but I immediately suspected some kind of irregularity) that this might be a place where I could acquire some ancient artefact, but on reflection, I realised that the man would not be handing me the map quite so openly if he were breaking the law: no precautions, no secrecy at all. He might as well have been selling potatoes. I hadn't the faintest idea what it was, but I bought it nevertheless. I paid very little for it, but judging by the profusion of thanks I received, the amount was satisfactory.'

'The following day I showed the map to the boatman. He knew what it was, and repeated certain words and names to me, but despite his efforts to explain things, more through sign language than anything else, I was still in the dark. As you, who know me so well, must surely suspect, my curiosity was now piqued beyond belief. I set off immediately, following the path marked in red on the map – and I must admit it wasn't too inaccurate. After I'd been walking for almost three hours, the house came into view. It was a very peculiar house; it looked like the architect was under the influence of alcohol when he designed it. As I got closer, I could see a small crowd of people waiting patiently outside. All those people were obviously there for a reason, but I hadn't the faintest idea what I was doing there. Nevertheless, I sat down under a tree next to a fat woman holding a basket and waited like everybody else. After me, others came. On arrival, they would ring the bell, and watch as the others shook their heads, indicating that ringing the bell was a waste of time.

After a while, a young woman emerged from the house, olive-skinned with long, wavy, dark hair. She addressed the crowd in a curt, peremptory voice at which everyone got to their feet and a few of them left. Some vacillated between staying and leaving, and some of them eventually left. But the majority stayed firmly in place. I did too. Later, she reappeared, and this time, without saying anything, pointed to the fat woman sitting next to me and beckoned her across. She almost felled me in her haste to get to her feet! The others were clearly disappointed, and gradually started to leave. I still had no idea what was going on, and decided to linger. The fat woman soon came out again, basket on her arm. When she saw me she smiled cheerfully and waved with her free hand. After she had gone, I was alone.

'The sun started to sink in the sky, and I thought that unless I wanted to spend the night on the mountains, I had better head back. Now that I think about it, I wasn't that worried because I did have a torch, a telescope and a compass with me. I pulled out my telescope to examine the surrounding area, and while I was looking at the map, trying to make out the mountain range I'd seen on the way up, the young girl came out again and began to speak in that same stern manner – only this time she was addressing me exclusively. It was clear that she wanted me to leave, but all of a sudden, she stopped talking and I saw that she was staring at my telescope, her eyes bursting with curiosity.'

'You did not, I trust, allow such an opportunity to go unexploited?' said the baron with mounting interest in T. Rosenmann's narrative.

'I quickly handed it to her and told her to look through it. I cannot describe the primitive shrieks of delight she made as she put her eye to the lens – her terrified father came rushing out to see what had happened to her! Satisfied that nothing untoward was taking place, he took a long look through it too and then invited me in.

'At first, conversation was awkward, but fortunately he had a smattering of French and Italian and we gradually established a code of communication. He showed me round his library, obviously taking great pride in it; admittedly it was rather impressive for a village house. He pulled out a few books on astronomy he thought would be of interest to me – reasonable when you consider that he had just seen me wondering around with a telescope. Father and daughter were both very pleasant, and despite the language barrier, very talkative. They asked me what I did, and I told them I was a professor, which encouraged them to take down even more volumes from the shelves, this time titles related to my area of expertise. But it was getting late. I made to leave, but they wouldn't hear of it. They were adamant that I should not walk in the dark alone, and the daughter, with staggering spontaneity, grabbed me by the hand, all but begging me to stay.

'Only a short while before she'd been so desperate to get rid of you!'

'Yes. Their goodwill made me feel very privileged. But I still didn't know what it was that had people flocking to their door.'

'Go on.'

'The young girl had prepared a wonderful, thick soup out of soured yoghurt and spearmint, and we all sat down to eat. I spent the entire meal trying to discover something that would help me solve the mystery of what these people did, but in vain. The answer, as I will explain, came of its own accord.'

'After soup, we were served warm bread rolls with olive oil and sugar. When those were finished, the girl cleared the table and the father and I started a discussion about the various places he had visited, inasmuch as a discussion could take place, that is. I was very surprised to hear that the man was so well travelled (unless of course he was lying to me, and everything he knew about these places he had gleaned from his books). At some point he signalled something to his daughter who instantly understood what he wanted and got up to get it. She returned with a tiny little tray holding a narrow tube-like glass filled with honey and three small twigs, which had been stripped down with a knife. She placed the tray on the table and started talking angrily, in a tone recalling her earlier appearances in the garden. Her father, trying to help me understand, pointed to the glass holding the honey and said: '*Tutti giorno problema!*'

'In a flash I understood what all the fuss was about – honey. It made me wonder. Rodakis (that was the man's name) tasted it first. He dipped a twig into the glass. His daughter did the same. I used the third twig. And then…'

T. Rosenmann stopped and smiled on one side of his face, his ear twitching as he did.

'Then what happened?'

'Baron, quite simply, all my doubts vanished, as yours will. I could see why all those people had been queuing up outside. I could see why people were selling maps showing the way up to the house. I could see why the fat lady had come out with such a huge grin on her face. I could see why the glass was so narrow.'

'I take it the honey was tasty.'

'Very. Although "tasty" is hardly the word I would have used. Properly prepared, one of your geese might be described as be "tasty".'

'How would you describe it?'

'I'd been wondering about that myself: What is the *mot juste*? And then it came to me. The only word that even begins to describe the full merits of the honey is the name its creator gave it, the name printed on the label.'

'I asked you about that earlier, and you didn't answer me. What does it say?'

T. Rosenmann sounded the word written on the label: An-ge-li-co.

The baron repeated the syllables and asked:

'And what does "An-ge-li-co" mean?'

'Angelico,' explained T. Rosenmann, 'means "made by angels" – or "made for angels". A little flowery, I know, but the islanders,' he continued, 'never refer to it as honey; honey is what they spread on their bread, or use in their baking. They always call it Angelico.'

'And you paid through the nose for it. Forgive me if I seem rude, but how much did you spend on my gift? I think my curiosity is justified in this case.'

'Let me explain. After this unexpected development, I tried to ask Rodakis a few things about his production methods, and he did try to answer me but, because of the language problem, I am not sure whether I understood him correctly. Basically, for the last four years, this man has been successfully feeding his bees on a particular combination of plants, and this is the result. He produces very little each year and as you can imagine, that makes Angelico very scarce and very expensive. I subsequently found out from the locals that Angelico's reputation has spread abroad, and is making Rodakis wealthier and wealthier with each passing day.'

The baron began to look at the tiny bottle resting in his palm in a different light.

'Did he by any chance reveal the magic combination to you – seeing that he took such a shine to you?'

'You must be joking,' laughed T. Rosenmann. 'That combination is written down somewhere in his head (that's what he gave me to understand by knocking his forehead with his hand). Nobody else knows what it is.'

At that moment, the loud squawks of two duelling geese were

heard overhead.

'Insufferable creatures,' said the baron, irritated. 'They'll have to seek employment elsewhere. That's final. I'm filling the lake with water lilies instead. Pity about the…'

'The what?'

'That you have be so frugal with it and eat it from the tip of a twig.'

'That's not such a serious drawback. Angelico is not something you eat to satisfy your hunger. The satisfaction it brings can be attained from a single drop. Imagine what would happen if you placed a full teaspoon in your mouth. You would swallow most of it, and it would go to waste. The satisfaction would have come from the tiniest amount left stuck on your palate. It is a pure, sensual pleasure aimed neither at the throat nor the stomach. In fact, that little bottle I brought you should last you a good few months. The taste lingers on, believe me. You'd probably accuse me of exaggeration if I told you that I could still feel traces of the taste circulating around my mouth the next morning.'

'So did you end up spending the night there?'

'Yes. I rose early, but they were already up. I thanked them warmly for their hospitality and thought the least I could do was give the girl my telescope as a token of my appreciation. She jumped up and down in delight and handed me a small bottle of honey she'd kept back for me. Now it was my turn to jump for joy but I restrained myself. I kept half for myself and transferred the other half into the bottle you're holding – the label is my own design.'

As he spoke, T. Rosenmann lifted the lid and extracted a long, thin silver needle from a concealed opening inside it.

'Won't you try some?'

'I can't wait. But not here. Not with this dreadful row going on,' said the baron, nodding in the direction of the lake.

The two men stood up and walked towards the mansion. Before they reached the door, the baron asked:

'You know, you never did tell me the name of the island where you had this extraordinary experience!'

T. Rosenmann mumbled the name, without moving his lips.

'I beg your pardon?' said the perplexed baron.

'I didn't say anything,' replied T. Rosenmann, all innocence, adding, 'Unfortunately it has slipped my mind. It'll come back to me.'

The baron could have sworn that he had heard something. A name.

Many people were struck by the parallels between Rodakis's sudden rise to wealth and that of his father's a few decades earlier. The obvious similarity was the source of their respective fortunes, but with one important difference: the effect it had on the two men. S. Rodakis put his money to work in order to secure a more comfortable existence for himself: he bought land; built a big new house; married off his daughter – all of which brought significant changes to his life. His son, on the other hand, never gave a thought to either investment or expansion, and he never replaced anything. Thus this explosion of wealth into his life did not have the slightest impact on his many sacrosanct rituals and habits.

Nevertheless, as Angelico became more and more popular with each passing year, he made sure the price reflected demand. It got to the point where everyone started accusing him of exploitation and profiteering – and with reason – because even the tiniest quantity cost a small fortune. When Father Chryssanthos, delegated to represent a number of outraged customers, broached the subject, Rodakis merely argued that his honey was purchased on a totally voluntary basis and it was not as though he held the monopoly on a staple. The priest, beyond the bee-keeper's modest donation for the orphans jingling in his cassock pocket, came away empty-handed.

The only refurbishment that Rodakis carried out was to the

back storeroom, the only part of the house that had always resisted any attempt to impose order on. It looked shabby and neglected. He thought the space could be put to better use: he could keep his collection of stones there, for example – not that he owned any such collection, but that didn't rule out the possibility in the future; he could even install a research laboratory in there – not that he had any research projects in mind, but something might occur to him at a later date. The only thing he was certain of was that this room should be dedicated to a new project, and once all the old junk inside had been cleared and basic renovation work been completed, the inspiration for a project would soon come.

When he went to make a preliminary inspection (who knows how long it had been since he had last set foot in there), he had to apply a lot of force to the door, and even then only managed to open it wide enough to squeeze through, and scrape his nose in the process. The sight that greeted him was exactly what he had been expecting: a picture of total disarray. Even the stench of dead animal wafting into his nostrils came as no surprise.

He set to work, not expecting to find anything of value. He was proved wrong when one of Vaya's two trunks emerged from behind a heavy bundle of dried out branches. (The other trunk had long since been taken up to her bedroom and was used to store Rosa's and her own clothes.) This one had stayed down here. Judging by the ease with which he pulled it out, it was probably empty. He opened it: an old sheet was spread across the bottom, on which two dead centipedes had found their final resting place. Under the sheet were various old papers – letters – some loose, others inside envelopes, and a book called *Beloved Thorns*. One quick look was enough to establish that it was one of those romantic novels he despised so much, written by some French woman. The heroine was a woman who adored collecting thorns: thorns which clearly had some kind of 'allegorical meaning', symbolising the suffering the heroine would encounter in life. It was almost impossible to reconcile Vaya's tough personality with this kind of book – this one even had dried leaves and thorns secreted away between its pages. The mere thought of Vaya with tears in her eyes reading about the suffering of a sickly young girl almost made him laugh out loud.

He turned to the letters. Vaya was dead. That, coupled with the fact that the letters were not sealed, extinguished any reservations he may have had. Most of them were signed 'Nectaria'. Nectaria was Vaya's trusted cousin, the one who had taken her in and had had '*I will find you*' carved above her front door. One of the letters read:

'I was so happy to hear that you have at last found somewhere to live, and from what you say, he sounds like a good man, so: Praise be to God! But please be careful, and if you want my advice, you'll keep yourself to yourself. They've been back, those two policemen. I told them the same thing again – that I had no idea where you were. They'll give up sooner or later. I don't want you to worry about anything except the child.'

Elsewhere he read:

'For the time being, the most sensible thing would be for you to write to me at the address we talked about, always anonymously, and I'll write to you care of the priest. Now that he's heard your confession, there is no way he can talk. I just hope that he doesn't read my letters on the sly before he passes them on to you. Father, if you are reading these lines, all I can say is: May God forgive you.'

And elsewhere:

'I am very upset as I write these words. He was here. At least he was calm. He said that he had lost one child but had gained another in its place and if you decide that you want to see him, he says he'll visit you and the child, wherever you may be. He gave his word that he wouldn't turn you in to the police. That's what he said, but I don't know if you can trust him. I stuck to my story: I don't know; I don't know; I don't know anything…

Remember that lawyer I told you about? He was here yesterday too. He told me that I mustn't touch the door until the police have sent round their expert to examine the carving to see how old it is, because he says that if you can prove that you left because of his threats that would be an extenuating circumstance.'

Elsewhere:

'When you first wrote to me about the honey, it all sounded so silly. I wondered how the man could be so naïve. But you tell me that it's all going very well. I hope it is. The ends justify the means, as they say. You ask about my health. I'm well, but I have to make sure I drink plenty of water on account of my kidneys.

If you stay away for at least another year, things will have calmed down a lot. The police haven't been round for ages. Of course I am not telling you to come back, but we could find a little house somewhere in some other town for you to move into with the child. When people start to forget. But if you can stay there on the island, as you say you can, you should.

It's already been six years. Imagine that. Tell me – is there nothing more to your relationship with that man than the fact that you are living under the same roof? Tell me more.'

Reading this and passages like it, Rodakis realised that Vaya had kept the truth from him all those years. It was not, as she had claimed, her husband who had been hunting her down on account of the sinful relationship she had with his father – it was the police and the father himself. As far as he could tell, she was wanted for the murder of her husband. This was the only reasonable conclusion anyone reading those letters could draw. Rodakis's picture of Vaya unravelled in an instant. The only element that remained unchanged from Vaya's account was that her father-in-law, not her husband, was Rosa's father.

There were three more letters – he took a quick look at them and decided they were three of the thirty-three she had sent her father-in-law, and which he had later returned. Rodakis did not read those letters.

It dawned on him that all the years they had been together,

he had never gained her trust sufficiently for her to tell him the truth. In essence, they had always been strangers to each other. It also occurred to him that the only person who knew the truth (or at least part of it) and who was in a position to enlighten him was the priest. He set off in search of him, to demand the facts, which he felt he had a right to, but half way there, he thought better of it and turned back.

What difference did it make now? Whatever the facts of Vaya's life, for him they were no more than circumstances – circumstances which, one after the other, had led her to his door. A web of fate, bringing death to her; strength and profit to him.

The Site and the surrounding area, which was known by the same name, had established itself in the minds of the islanders as a holy place. But its holy aspect, instead of promoting a sense of tranquillity and piety, gave rise to indefinable fear and superstition. For that reason, it did not attract many pilgrims; only the occasional oddball – relatives mostly, leaving offerings and prayers in the hope that they were helping their loved ones recover their wits, or the use of their limbs, or in other cases, release them from the powers of witchcraft and diabolical possession.

The monastery was very prosperous; its wealth had increased over the centuries, although the number of monks who entered it had not. It was common knowledge that this was due more to the financial acumen of its successive abbots than to divine grace. Its fortune was made up of priceless ecclesiastical vessels, worked in gold and precious stones, gospels of inestimable value, icons and papyri, as well as a great deal of land which it leased to farmers who paid a sizable proportion of their harvest in rent. The abbot only held onto whatever produce was necessary to cover the monastery's needs; the rest was sold on his behalf by various wholesalers who kept a share of the sale in turn. The merchants claimed that the monastery in general and the abbot in particular were some of the toughest negotiators in the business, not just because they were very demanding, but because the heavy spiritual atmosphere of the room where these dealings took place, the piercing looks of the monks, both those present and their predecessors who were immortalised in monastery icons exerted a psychological pressure on them which would reliably subdue their objections.

It was rumoured that the monastery also conducted a number of business deals behind closed doors. With a deal of this kind in mind, Rodakis reached the foot of the Site hill. He had decided some time ago only to sell honey harvested in the spring when all the plants were in flower at the same time, as it was only then that the formula was correctly applied. While this gave him scope for hiking up his high prices, it automatically limited his output, so he needed to find a way to extend production within this very short season. There was only one solution; he would have to increase the number of hives, but this would require a larger area, both for additional hives and additional plants.

Rodakis could afford to buy any piece of land he wanted, wherever he wanted it; but he wanted the land adjoining his own, and had good reasons for wanting it. One reason was that he was nervous of relocating; he feared that doing so might jinx his luck. The other reason was practical, related to the fact that this land was part of the burnt woodland area, and the only things growing there were weeds, so the bees would automatically congregate on the plants and flowers that he chose to plant there.

The land belonged to the monastery; after the big fire, the monastery came forward in a spirit of charity, offering to buy up much of the burnt land from owners who were no longer able to make money from selling wood. Rodakis did not anticipate any difficulty persuading the abbot to sell him a plot of charred land, but had decided that he would pay whatever price was asked.

A monk showed him to the back of the monastery, to a cool balcony where the abbot was sitting perched on a hard, high-backed wooden chair, which looked extremely uncomfortable.

His eyelids were closed and Rodakis, assuming that he was asleep, remained silent, but the old man's hoarse voice was heard almost immediately:

'That didn't take long; I wasn't expecting you so soon.'

Convinced that the abbot was still somewhere between a state of dreaming and a state of wakefulness, and that these words were directed at an interlocutor in a dream rather than at him, he hesitated before he spoke.

'I am S. Rodakis's son.'

'I know who you are.'

'I don't know if I have come at an inconvenient time; there is something I would like us to discuss.'

'Do you believe we have something to discuss?'

Rodakis did not really understand what the abbot meant by that, and put it down to the fact that he had woken so abruptly.

'I have always found it interesting to listen to the reasons people think they have for coming here. Some say they suddenly feel the urge to make a pilgrimage, others claim to have seen a sign in their dreams. Others – like yourself – are suddenly inspired to come and discuss the most bizarre subjects under the sun with me.'

'My case is slightly different. I really do have something to discuss with you, and it has nothing to do with either my imagination or any kind of inspiration.'

'Yes, you have come in response to my summons,' replied the abbot in a calm voice, and while there was nothing discernibly hostile in his tone, Rodakis felt a wall of intransigence building up between them, which did not bode well for the beginning of his negotiations, so instead of arguing, he asked:

'What summons?'

The abbot did not answer.

'Had I received such a summons, I would never pretend that I was here on some other business. Why would I do such a thing?'

'Because you were unaware of it. The summons is issued and received by the mind; all that is felt is an urge to come here, so everybody tries to rationalise it and looks for a reason, and, understandably, believes that reason to be true.'

'Do you mean to say that the reason I am standing here now is because you summoned me, and not because of the matter I wish to discuss with you?'

'Precisely.'

'On the other hand,' said Rodakis trying to maintain as neutral a tone as possible, 'this matter, this pretext you could say, is not something that has just occurred to me. I've been thinking about it for a year now. Long before your summons, I imagine.'

'I summoned you last night.'

'How do you explain that?' asked Rodakis, confident that he had demolished the abbot's preposterous arguments.

'How do you explain that you have been considering the matter for a year and you only happened to come and see me now, the morning after my summons? Do you consider this to be a coincidence? Or perhaps you think I am lying when I tell you that I summoned you last night?' asked the abbot, reading Rodakis's mind with some accuracy.

'Of course not.'

A few moments passed before either of them spoke.

'We could of course reach a compromise: let us assume that there really is something I need to discuss with you, but it is because of your summons that I am here today rather than some other day.'

'As you wish,' replied the abbot, knowing full well that the only thing the man standing before him wanted was to get this over with, and move on to his own business.

For the first time, Rodakis met the old man's gaze. All of a sudden, he was under the impression that he had seen his face somewhere recently; the image was very fresh but a minor lapse in his memory kept him from placing it. However, only seconds earlier, he would have put his hand in the fire and sworn that the only time he had seen this man before was many years ago, when as a young boy, he had come up to the Site with his father and sister. This sudden impression was akin to the feeling people get when they see someone they know and suddenly remember that they dreamt about them the night before, only then recalling that they had the dream at all. All this unsettled him, and made him wonder whether the abbot really had appeared to him in some dream or vision which he had immediately forgotten, and whether this was the real reason he had made his way up to the monastery that day. This dampened his original impulse to settle the question of the land as quickly as possible and leave. Now he was more curious to know why he had been summoned here in this preternatural manner in the first place. But the abbot was one step ahead of him.

'What did you want to see me about?'

'I'd like you to sell me some land belonging to the monastery.'

'You want to buy some land. Original! Really? Where?'

'It's in the burnt area. I'm interested in the plot adjacent to mine.'

'Where you keep your bees?'

'That's right.'

'You're expanding.'

'Exactly.'

'Take it. It's yours.'

Rodakis was disconcerted by this offer; the abbot was not exactly famous for his generosity, and he suspected that there were strings attached to this magnanimous offer.

'I'm not asking for a gift. I would like to buy it.'

'If you don't want to accept it as a gift, you can have unlimited and unrestricted use of it. But if you insist on paying for it, I won't stop you. Decide on a price and it's yours.'

Rodakis chose the latter option. Their discussion was interrupted by the arrival of a monk with a bulging forehead, who bent over and whispered something in the abbot's ear, as if to remind him of a prior obligation. The abbot listened, nodded and turned to Rodakis, saying:

'We'll continue this discussion some other time. For the moment, if you'd care to accompany the brother here, he will show you how our work is progressing.'

He rose to his feet and walked off with an agility and speed that someone who had seen him sitting down would never have suspected him capable of. The monk escorted Rodakis out and led him up to the hill where building work was in progress, to the Site itself, making a point of stressing what a rare opportunity this was, and that it was a sign of that he was in favour with the abbot.

Work had started up on the Site at least two hundred years before. At that time there was absolutely nothing in the area apart from a cave at the foot of the hill, which was really nothing more that a rift in the rocks, making a welcoming recess for snakes and other creatures. An anchorite, who had dedicated his life to God in this deserted place, the most deserted spot on the island, had also made his home there. In addition to day-long prayer he had devoted himself to the task of opening up another room at the back of the cave, smaller than the natural opening, and about the size of the sanctuary in most churches. The inside of the hill was rocky, so he had to work by chiselling away at it slowly, his only tools a piece of iron with a crude point and a few stones.

The anchorite was not disheartened by his slow progress; on the contrary it steeled his self-discipline and his concentration. However, hardship and hostile conditions proved stronger than he was and after a few years the exhausted hermit gave up the ghost before he could complete the task. Although unfinished, the results of his labours were in every respect admirable. A small corridor, no longer than a generous stride and no wider than the back of the anchorite who had dug it, led into the room he had created. This small antechamber afforded good protection from the elements, but not enough to prevent the intense cold from killing the anchorite one fateful winter. The four walls of the room appeared to have been worked at painstakingly, with unlimited patience. The thousands of blows from the hermit's primitive tools were visible on their uneven surfaces like broad brushstrokes on a canvas which announce the precise size and type of brush used in their execution – with the exception of one section of crude, jagged edges and protrusions, the part he did not live to finish. The ceiling was domed, which must have caused great inconvenience in the making, as he would have had to climb onto some kind of support to reach it. Nevertheless, he had managed to forge a very even arch, like a cupola, and had also carved a cross into it. With the floor, in contrast to the walls and ceiling, he had tried to achieve a completely smooth surface, but had not quite succeeded. Years later, his bones were found on that same floor; a hunter discovered them by chance.

The hunter explained how his dog had led him into the cave (it did not go into the second room). There, filled with awe, before him he saw human remains, lying between two icons and a pile of dried grass. The most shocking thing about his story was what he discovered on leaving the cave. His ear, which had been suffering from profound deafness ever since he had taken part in a battle – he was in the artillery – regained its hearing. He became aware of this a few metres away from the cave by the buzzing of a vicious bee apparently anxious to sample his earwax. Word of this incident soon got round, and the belief that the cave contained holy relics quickly took root. The local worthies immediately decided to build a shrine next to the cave in which to house the sacred bones and make them accessible for worship.

At about the same time, a group of monks, some of them for reasons of irreconcilable dogmatic differences (but by no means all, whatever they said) broke away from the monastic community on the neighbouring island, and made their appearance. They were looking for a new place, pure and unspoiled, a suitable place for them to regain their faith and their love for the monastic ideal. The position of the cave and the hill which, thanks to the geological features of the surroundings, made it seem like it had somehow detached itself from this world and existed in a vacuum, with no associations or memories, good or bad, attached to it beyond the sainted figure of the old anchorite who once lived there. It was the answer to their prayers.

Nobody imagined that those monks, with their cadaverous faces and filthy, fraying cassocks, who arrived one day on some barely seaworthy old vessel, had a veritable treasure concealed in their knapsacks. Treasures, books, vessels, as well as the gold they had brought to cover necessary expenditures – and they were prepared to guard it with their lives. Their wealth only became apparent when they started buying materials and equipment and hiring builders to start work on the church and the new monastery next to it.

When the building was finished and their new life had settled into a regular pattern, one of the monks approached the abbot, asking for permission to finish the work on the last wall of the cave. The only thing he was worried about was the possibility that his abbot would refuse to allow anyone to interfere with the Site in view of the fact that the anchorite had been canonised – if only unofficially. The abbot, however, had serious doubts concerning the sanctity of the relics lying inside the gold inlaid box in the centre of the church, and gave his blessing to the young monk without giving the matter much thought. The monk set to work without delay, but as soon as he did, another monk approached the abbot with a similar request: to complete the anchorite's work by opening up a new chamber on the side of the unfinished wall. The abbot considered the matter a little more carefully this time, and gave his consent, which was conditional on the approval of the first monk, whose hammering and banging had already started to disturb the peace of the hillside. This proposal did not please the first monk, but he relented and the two monks threw themselves into the job of opening the new wall together. Their example was the envy of many, and soon all the monks were asking for permission to contribute to this challenging task.

The abbot gave his blessing to them all without exception, reasoning that he should take advantage of this sudden spirit of diligence to create a few secure rooms in which their treasures could be stored, or better, some cell-chambers, to which a monk could retreat to find peace, or even be sent to for correction. If nothing else, they could provide useful refuges in the event of a pirate raid.

The monks worked zealously away at the hard rock. They chiselled holes in the unfinished wall and opened up a tunnel that was like a corridor running through the heart of the hill. After that, everyone pursued their own path. Some wanted to work in groups, others preferred to be alone. Each group functioned independently. With the exception of the tunnel, which was a joint effort, there was no basic plan, and everybody was free to determine what shape the section they were working on would take. Nobody interfered with anybody else's decisions to make a section large or small, square or circular, to give it a raised or a sunken floor. This freedom focused the monks' imagination and creativity, transforming a laborious task, which, under different circumstances, even the most hardened galley slave would have baulked at, into something genuinely rewarding. Most of the monks from this first batch only set down their tools when their aging hands refused to submit to such exertions and it was time to hand over to younger hands.

The prospect of being able to work in the underbelly of the hill encouraged several young men to enter the monastery, so the tradition was kept up by subsequent generations of monks. Over time, the inside of the hill gradually evolved into a complex edifice resembling a gigantic ants' nest known as the Site – not a literal meaning, as it did not actually describe something that was being built or constructed, but something that was being excavated.

Despite the lack of coordination with which the work progressed, there was one inviolable rule all concerned were required to respect: security. For this reason, a second entrance was never opened up and none of the light or ventilation shafts were accessible from the outside. Furthermore, without spoiling its natural shape, the entrance to the cave had been skilfully modified to accommodate a solid, double iron door, secured with heavy chains at night, turning the Site into an impregnable fortress.

One of the abbots, renowned for his wise sayings, commented that the result of the sweat of all those monks over the years was not simply the achievement of skill and patience, but a map on which the personalities of those who had laboured there was marked out and immortalised. The self-denial and fortitude of the holy anchorite; the vanity of the monk who first hewed out twenty-five steps in the rock before starting to dig out his own room; the feebleness of certain others who preferred to be given orders, or to finish off loose ends left behind by others; the perfectionism of the monk determined to achieve the ultimate smooth finish on his wall; the artistry of another who instead of making his own room, decided to decorate other rooms, carving Christian symbols, geometric patterns and honeysuckle into the walls and ceilings. The imprint of their spirits was inaccessible to the eyes of the world as the Site only ever opened its gates in exceptional circumstances.

Rodakis was clearly one such exception. His entry into the Site was proof of this and the monk with the bulging forehead showing him around had already commented on it.

They spent a long time wandering around inside the dark bowels of the hill. The monk was not in a hurry; on the contrary, he was happy to answer all of Rodakis's questions and to share all his knowledge about each room as well as detail the chronology of the work. He told him that the excavation work would soon come to an end and they would be forced to halt operations altogether because of a concern that further disturbance to the hill would affect the stability of the entire structure. They had already cut back the number of monks working inside the Site, and they were working only a few metres from the top of the hill, if his calculations were right.

The fantastic picture he had of the Site in his mind bore no relation to the reality of the place. The most astonishing thing about the place was the obvious lack of any coherent plan. After a certain point, there were a number of turnings you could take; some were dead-ends; others, although they looked like diversions, actually joined up with other passageways. But there was no main artery leading from the entrance to the back. When he said as much, the monk explained that this was the consequence of a decision not to adhere to any particular plan. Something else that made an impression on him was that besides a few benches in some of the rooms the place was completely bare, and these rudimentary stone benches looked like a natural extension of the stone walls anyway, not independent pieces of furniture.

Valuables and holy vessels were stored in rooms that had been specially sealed behind heavy iron bars, and were not opened, even for their visitor, who had to content himself with a very brief glimpse through the bars. These were the largest and most carefully presented rooms, boasting the most elaborate ornamentation. They had small circular light shafts bored through several layers of rock through which bundles of feeble light reached the room. The opening to the light shaft was covered by a sort of wire mesh to keep insects and other wildlife at bay. The room serving as the monastery library naturally attracted Rodakis's attention, even though he estimated that there could not have been more than a hundred books standing on its concave shelves. Certain of the smaller cells were also behind bars: the monk, being deliberately vague, explained that they were 'put to various uses'.

As they ascended the interior of the hill, the sound of the chisels hammering away at the stone intensified. When they arrived at the scene of all this activity, Rodakis, in the light shining from the monks' lanterns as well as the one his own guide was holding, counted five silhouettes. Two of them were up on wooden ladders, adding the finishing touches to the ceiling of a round room while another pair were still in the early stages of work on two facing cells leading off the round room. The fifth, barely visible at the back of the room, was making a further staircase.

'These are going to be the last steps,' explained the monk, ' – they will lead to the last room. The last room will be the first to be constructed in a communal effort involving all the brothers working from a common plan. It will be built as an act of thanksgiving – our thanks to God for allowing us to see this task to completion. If our calculations are accurate, the ceiling will be slightly lower than the highest point of the hill: this gave us the idea of opening up an enormous circular fanlight in the middle of the ceiling. This room will be a place of prayer; whoever comes here will be able to look directly at heaven as he prays.'

While he was talking, the monk working on the construction of the last staircase, his back to them all the while, turned to see where the whispering was coming from. The light from the lantern behind him did not reach his face, which was almost invisible in the darkness. Something told Rodakis that he was looking at Paschalis, his old assistant. He took a step towards him, but his guide motioned to him to leave, and later explained that it was forbidden to disturb the monks while they were working because work was always accompanied by meditation.

When they emerged into daylight, the monk announced that he had to return to his duties, and that his visitor was welcome to wait in the orchard until the abbot called him back to conclude their discussion.

After a couple of hours, another monk appeared and invited

him to join them for their evening meal. The abbot was not present at the table. He scanned the room in search of the monk he had thought was Paschalis, but he couldn't see either Paschalis or anyone resembling him at any of the three tables in the refectory. At the end of the meal, the monk with the bulging forehead approached Rodakis and told him that the abbot was indisposed following an episode of vertigo, in view of which their appointment would have to be postponed until the following morning.

He invited Rodakis to spend the night in the guestroom. When he considered that this would mean that Rosa would be left alone without warning, he declined. However, when he took into account how important the meeting with the abbot was, and that if he left, he would only have to make the long journey back again the following morning, he reconsidered.

A novice with a pleasant face showed him to his quarters.

'Don't take offence if the bed smells a bit damp – we're not accustomed to receiving visitors.'

He wished him a good night and made to leave, but then turned and said:

'The water in the jug is fresh, by the way.'

Rodakis got undressed, drank a little water and went to sleep.

A disagreeable chill woke him in the early hours. He groped around in the dark for his blanket but instead he found his hand sinking into dry straw, and realised that he was no longer in the bed he fallen asleep in the night before. His fingers felt along a large stone surface, wondering where he was and how he had ended up outside. He looked up but could make out neither the stars nor the moon. As his eyes yielded no clues, he emitted a loud cry, hoping to be able to tell from the way it pierced the silence what sort of place he was in.

The distant echo made him think of something else, which

proved correct. After a few blind steps taken with his arms stretched out in front of him, he touched the cold iron bars of a door – of the kind he had seen a few hours earlier in some of the cells inside the Site – bolted.

The pressure on his head and his eyelids, the weakness in all his limbs, as well as a slight numbness in the soles of his feet made him suspect that he had been drugged, moved and, possibly, imprisoned inside the Site. The anaesthetic, he thought, might have been hidden in his food, or in the water the novice had brought to the guestroom. As to why any of this was happening, he was completely in the dark.

At first light, a blurred horizontal line appeared on the wall facing the iron door. Rodakis went to look at it up close and saw that it was coming from a crack in the wooden covering of the light shaft. Removing the covering, he felt the morning light and the fresh air beating down on his face. The width of the shaft (basically a small tunnel) was four, at a pinch five metres, and despite the fact that its square opening in the wall was quite large, it gradually tapered off into a small round hole no more than twenty centimetres in diameter; impossible, even for a small child, to get out through.

The light, slowly intensifying, gave some answers to Rodakis's questions. He could now see the straw he had felt on waking, see that it was a mattress he had obviously been dumped onto. His clothes lay folded a bit further away. He also found a lamp filled with oil, which he would have lit if he'd seen it earlier.

The cell was divided into two separate sections that communicated through a narrow archway. Rodakis lit the lantern and went through to the second section, which had no light shaft and was drenched in darkness. It too had an iron door, which was predictably locked. He then recalled that on his tour the previous day the monk with the bulging forehead had mentioned this cell, and had said that it was called the Error Room. Originally there had been two independent chambers, worked on concurrently by two monks, but as the result of an error of judgement on the part of at least one of them, the two monks came face to face as they chiselled through the rock that separated them. Instead of rectifying the mistake they decided to give this accidental breach an arcuated form and that is how the double room came to be known as the Error Room. Later, monks who went astray would be isolated for a spell in there for prayer and contemplation. The monk did not specify whether errant monks freely undertook this isolation or whether it was a punitive measure imposed on them by the monastery. One thing was clear – the choice of this room for this purpose was inspired by its name.

Alone with his thoughts inside a stone cell, striking out fruitlessly at the hard walls, Rodakis heard a key in the iron lock. Three figures slipped in while a fourth locked the door from the outside. As the three monks came down through the arch one by one and entered the lighted chamber, he was able to see their faces. The first was none other than this guide of the previous day. Next to appear was the abbot, and behind him was the monk who had invited him to dinner and had sat next to him during the meal (and had conceivably slipped a sleeping pill into his food).

For a moment nothing was said. The three of them stood there looking at Rodakis and Rodakis looked at the three of them in turn. His eyes rested on the bleak calm of the abbot's eyes.

'I hear that you have been feeling unwell. I trust you are better today?' asked Rodakis.

'I had a very trying night, but yes, I am feeling better.'

'I also had an unusual night. I fell asleep in one place and woke up in another.'

'I am aware of that.'

'Why am I here? I won't ask how I got here. But why am I here?'

'First of all, I must ask you to forgive us for moving you here and for the way it happened. The responsibility for this rests entirely with me and no one else. If I have done wrong, once again, forgive me; I simply wanted to make sure that you did not leave before I had a chance to see you and for us to have our little talk.'

'But I came all this way to do precisely that.'

'Yes, yes, we've been over that.'

'It appears, however, that what you have to tell me is more important than what I have to tell you. Very well – I'm listening.'

To the astonishment of Rodakis, who once more was forced to marvel at the suppleness of the abbot, who had clearly preserved a youthful vigour inside his geriatric flesh, walked across to him and sat down on the straw mattress under the fanlight, motioning to the other two monks to go into the other chamber (not because he didn't want them to hear but because he wanted to be alone with the prisoner). Nothing was said for some time. Rodakis was worried that if he did not open his mouth, the silence would become interminable, and came straight to the point:

'I am imprisoned in a room you call the Error Room, used for the confinement of monks who fall into error. What am I to make of this? That I too have committed some crime which is in your view reprehensible and which makes me deserving of imprisonment?'

The abbot lowered his gaze and returned it to its previous level, determined to speak plainly too.

'Not on account of what you have done but on account of what you are about to do.'

'Can you read the future, old man? Are you some kind of clairvoyant?'

'I am frequently able to see into the future although I am no soothsayer.'

'So what is this error I am about to commit?'

'I do not wish to influence you.'

'Very well. Tell me why you summoned me? But I imagine that you will give me the same answer,' said Rodakis. And that was when a new, vague suspicion formed, soon to be confirmed by the abbot's words.

'I summoned you here because there is something I want to ask you. I would like you to sign over the formula for your honey to the monastery.'

All that could be heard in the Error Room for some time after that was the deep breathing of the monks waiting in the darkness, but soon even that stopped as they strained to work out what was going on in the adjoining chamber during this short silence. Eventually, Rodakis spoke.

'I see. And my refusal will be the error I am about to commit – or did you have something else in mind?'

The abbot did not reply.

'It certainly wouldn't take a clairvoyant to predict my response. Naturally I refuse. Why should I agree to this? I imagine this means that you will refuse to sell me that land. It doesn't really matter. The only thing I want now is to leave. My daughter's expecting me.'

One of the monks appeared in the archway, looked the abbot straight in the eye as though expecting some kind of signal, but the abbot merely gestured to him to go back and wait.

'You are treading on dangerous ground; you believe that you and you alone are master of your success, this phenomenal success you have been granted.'

'I have been granted nothing. Everything I have achieved I have achieved on my own, by dint of hard work. Ten years of hard work. And yes, I am master, the only master of my success. If it is not mine, who does it belong to?'

'Nothing belongs to us – not the fruits of our labours; not even the aptitude that we have for work, our skill, our inventiveness – all of these things are gifts from the Lord. That is why they are called 'gifts'. They are not really given in a strict sense – they are merely on loan to us. The time always comes for us to return them.'

'I am speechless,' confessed Rodakis. 'I have never heard anything so absurd in my life.'

The abbot smiled.

'There are many other things I could tell you that you would no doubt find even more absurd. There is much that the human mind is unable to grasp.'

'Do you mean that you were talking in all seriousness? You want to persuade me to make a gift of the most important thing that I have achieved in my life to the monastery, by trying to convince me that it doesn't really belong to me in the first place? And by taking me prisoner in this dungeon of yours to intimidate me?'

'I hope that I will manage to persuade you that signing over your secret formula to the monastery would be the single most significant action of your life. Much more important than the discovery itself.'

'And why, may I ask?'

'Because it would mean that you had subordinated personal gain to a higher purpose, to the glorification of the name of the Lord.'

'And not for the enrichment of the monastery, I suppose?' replied Rodakis, adopting the tranquil attitude the abbot had maintained throughout the conversation.

'That too, naturally,' he replied, showing no signs of embarrassment at the last comment. 'That too serves to glorify the name of the Lord, I assure you. But you are wrong; our purpose is not to enrich ourselves. We aim for something quite different.'

'Indeed!'

'Word of your honey reached me some time ago; I heard a great deal about it but didn't pay it any mind at the time; I dismissed it as exaggeration. We make our own honey here, very fine honey. But it has never had the reception yours got. So I decided to send Anthimos,' he said, raising his eyebrows in the direction of the inner chamber where the two monks were waiting out of sight. Rodakis could not work out which of the two monks Anthimos was. 'I decided to send Anthimos to bring me a sample. He had enormous difficulty getting hold of any and it cost him a great deal of money. But he did find some and thus I was able to form my own opinion.'

'Your impressions?'

'It has a property that sets it apart from other honeys, something other than the taste itself. I concluded as much from the verdict of others as well as my own. I cannot quite explain it, but it affects you, it influences your mood, arouses feelings in you. It acts on you – that's what makes it so special. Perhaps it takes different people differently. Anthimos, when he tried it, immediately recalled his old grandmother who used to feed him honey when he was a little boy, and tears welled up in his eyes. Remember?' called the abbot, and the monk who had appeared earlier re-emerged in the opening, nodding.

'Others,' continued the abbot while Anthimos slipped back into the darkness, 'said that when they tasted the honey they felt a unique sense of well-being, a wonderful spiritual reawakening. That is when it occurred to me, in conversation with another brother, that perhaps we could put this experience to use in the service of our faith.

I won't pretend that we did not experiment with this thought in mind. We left the island for a few days in search of people who had neither heard of you nor your honey, simple country people. We let them taste the honey, telling them that it was holy. Harvested from the place where a devout old anchorite led his saintly existence and came to his reward.'

'One lie after another,' said Rodakis out loud.

The abbot, who never heard anything he didn't want to hear, went on:

'It made a huge impression on them; some fell to their knees, making the sign of the cross; others asked for an immediate confession, others told us how they regretted abandoning the path of righteousness. They all greeted your fine creation as tangible proof of God's existence, and in that one minuscule drop we allowed to fall into their mouths they saw Him standing before them, and received it as if in communion.'

'And we saw how this power could be put to good use – supporting and inspiring faith in God. You were right to call it "Angelico". All of human creation, on reaching perfection, has something of the divine about it, and keeps hidden within it a small piece of God himself, and in some sense returns to him. You would do well to remember that.'

'Did it not trouble your conscience that you were promoting, as you put it, faith through deception? You and I both know very well that Angelico is not sanctified in any way. It's an exceptional product, yes, perhaps even the best honey ever made – but holy it is not.'

'Why should that trouble my conscience? If I had a piece of pure gold and wanted to sell it, but had a buyer who doubted its purity and I had to resort to tricks and lies to persuade him to buy it, that wouldn't mean that I had deceived him. Not essentially.'

Rodakis, who had momentarily stopped following the abbot's arguments, suddenly got to his feet and stood up in front of him. The abbot, still on the straw mattress, looked up at him in astonishment.

'I have listened very carefully to everything you have said, and I promise you that I will give the matter due consideration. But now I would like to leave. Tell them to open up.'

In the gap between the two chambers appeared the heads of the two monks. The abbot grabbed Rodakis's hand and pulled himself up.

'If you leave now, you will never come back. You will make the mistake of never returning. That you will give the matter due consideration – of that I am confident. I'll be back tomorrow,' he said, crossing the room.

Rodakis made to follow him. As he did, Anthimos entered and seized hold of him, almost winding him in the process, while the abbot slipped into the dark cell. When the lock clicked open, he disappeared, accompanied by the monk with the bulging forehead. When a second click was heard, a sign that the door had been relocked, Anthimos relaxed his grip on Rodakis.

The village priest had not been sleeping well for some time. His days were taken up with caring for the orphans and attending to his parochial duties, which left little time for reflection. At night, however, when everything had settled down, the profound silence encouraged his mind to wander and his spirit to falter, and after two or three hours of tossing and turning in his bed, Father Chryssanthos would leave the house and roam the narrow village streets like a ghost.

The need to reach a decision, a decision that would have an impact on other people's futures, was becoming increasingly urgent, a burden which he could only relieve by walking around at night. He would return at dawn, exhausted before the day had even started, but also relieved because he knew that daylight would blank out the image in his mind of that dark figure who had suddenly turned up and troubled his conscience. The only thing he could remember about the man was that his eyebrows could merge and then separate without losing their bow-like shape. The rest of his face was a blank. Perhaps this was understandable, considering that he had only seen him once and at night, in the church, and the light from the candles had cast more shadow than light on the man's face, throwing his eyebrows into relief as a result.

This was all many years ago. He had been round all the coffee houses in the harbour asking questions about a woman and a child (he didn't know whether it was a boy or a girl) turning up here looking for refuge. The only answer he got was that the locals were all peace-loving folk who didn't keep track of the comings and goings on the island. Somebody suggested that the right person to talk to about this sort of thing was the priest. The priest attached to the port insisted that nothing of the kind had been brought to his attention but suggested that he spoke to some of the priests up in the villages.

That is how the man appeared on Father Chryssanthos's doorstep later that evening. As the priest opened the door, he realised that he was looking at Rosa's real father – Vaya's father-in-law. Her confession forbade him from saying anything, but he knew that silence in this case would not be enough. If he invoked the sanctity of confession and said he could not betray Vaya's confidence, it would be tantamount to telling the man that she was in hiding in the village and it would only be a matter of time before he tracked her down. This particular confession required more than the customary silence; he would have to lie.

'No. No women with children have been round here. If they had, I'd have been the first to hear about it,' said Father Chryssanthos, realising that this was the first lie he had told for as long as he could remember. However, emboldened by his belief that lying in this case was a divine injunction, he sank deeper and deeper into sin, knowing that he had been forgiven beforehand.

'Strange woman with a child? Round here? Impossible! What would she be doing here anyway? This village is forty-four houses all told. That's not even forty-five. And I know what goes on in all of them – the good and the bad. A woman with a child? Unheard of! And there aren't any empty houses or guest houses or anything like that round here either.'

After a while, aiming his words straight at the gap between the man's eyebrows, he added:

'Why are you looking for this woman anyway – if you don't mind my asking.'

'She has got my child. And she's wanted for murder,' answered the man, forcing his eyebrows together.

Feigning surprise, the priest told the man that if he cared to leave a forwarding address, he would write to him in the remote event that he heard anything.

But this had taken place such a long time ago, and the priest, convinced that he had done the right thing, had never lost any sleep over it. He had never mentioned the visit to Vaya or Rodakis, judging the danger to have passed and thinking it pointless to go upsetting people unnecessarily.

But things were different now. Vaya was dead. Her death may not have been responsible for making him wonder whether he should get in touch with Rosa's real father (although it did release him to some degree from the bonds of confession), but this latest development – Rodakis's inexplicable disappearance – put a different light on the matter. For the second time, Rosa had watched a parent leave the house never to return. With her mother, everything was cleared up very quickly, albeit in the worst possible way, but this business with her father was much more mysterious. Several days had passed since the earth had opened up and swallowed him without trace. Some people said that he must have been set upon by the gang of thieves that appeared occasionally on the island; others suspected lions. Whatever the truth, the fact remained that Rodakis was missing, presumably dead.

In the light of these developments, Father Chryssanthos had to re-evaluate the entire matter. More than that, he had to confront the question of whether he had the right to deprive a little girl of her real father and leave her orphaned. This decision, whatever it would turn out to be, weighed heavily on him and kept him awake at night – until that night. As he walked through the square, past the vandalised statue of a life-size lion, he came to a decision.

Despite giving his word that he would return the next day, the abbot did not show his face for another four days. Rodakis remained locked inside the Error Room and Anthimos stayed there with him. Huddled in a corner of the dark cell, the monk made no attempt to strike up conversation with him. Now and again he would stick his head through the gap to make sure that his cellmate was all right. As soon as Rodakis saw him, he would make a dismissive gesture, and Anthimos would retreat into the darkness. However, there were occasions on which Rodakis would stick his own head through the gap to ask Anthimos if he knew when the abbot was expected, or else to protest about his absurd imprisonment. Anthimos made some sort of incoherent reply from which it was impossible to extract any meaning or information.

Every few hours, another monk would unlock the door to the dark cell, push a tray of food through and remove the two chamber pots. On hearing the key turn, Anthimos would block the gap with his bulky, powerful form thus precluding all thoughts of escape.

The only exchange between the men during those first days at the Site took place one evening when Anthimos – who slept directly on the stone floor, without even a rudimentary straw mattress – heard a strange panting noise from the neighbouring room, an anxious asthmatic sob, quite horrible to listen to. He quickly lit a candle (the only thing he had with him besides his Psalter) and went through the arch to where Rodakis slept to see what was going on.

'Rodakis – are you all right?' he asked shaking him lightly by the shoulder.

'Leave me alone,' answered Rodakis abruptly, now awake.

'I've been told to keep an eye on you and make sure you're all right. You are all right, aren't you?'

'When is the abbot coming?' – he saw his chance to ask the only question that really interested him.

'He'll be here. Maybe tomorrow. I don't know. Why were you wheezing like that earlier? You're not sick, are you?'

'No. I'm not sick. Now leave. Don't worry; I'm not about to drop dead. Sometimes my breathing stops in my sleep; but I usually survive. Now go away!'

Anthimos returned to his corner and blew out the candle. Soon Rodakis's voice was heard again in the darkness.

'What would have happened if I'd decided not to spend that first night here and had gone home instead?'

The echo of his voice faded into the silence and there was a long pause before Anthimos spoke.

'When?'

'That cursed day that I set foot in here. That afternoon I was given the choice of spending the night and going home. What would have happened if I'd decided to go home?'

'You couldn't have gone home. As soon as you arrived, the gates were locked and we were all put on the alert. It's perfectly simple – we wouldn't have let you go. The Error Room was made up for you a long time ago.'

Rodakis lit the lantern and went into the neighbouring chamber, the dark chamber, which after nightfall was really no darker than his own.

'Do you really believe that you can keep me imprisoned here like this? I have decided not to speak of this to anybody, and therefore there is no way that word of what your abbot tried to get his claws on will get out. What is the man intending to do to me? Keep me in here until the day I die?'

'I don't know,' replied Anthimos, apparently truthfully.

'My daughter will be looking for me.'

'Did you tell her you were coming up here?'

Before Rodakis had a chance to answer, Anthimos continued:

'Not that it matters. If anyone comes here looking for you, the abbot will quickly throw them off the scent. He'll say that you came here a long time ago, wanting to discuss the purchase of some land; that you stayed until late in the evening; had dinner with us; that we did all we could to persuade you to spend the night, but you left because you were anxious to get home to your daughter. The Lord only knows what happened to you on your way home in pitch darkness... Who would have reason to doubt the old man? Did you walk here?'

'I rode my mule.'

'He'll be somewhere roaming the mountains by now. Alive or dead, he'll be found, and everyone will take it as a sign that you are dead. Anyway, who would think to look for you here? Nobody ever comes down here except the brothers, and even if you screamed at the top of your lungs, nobody on the outside would hear you. He's thought of everything, the old man.'

'What a truly remarkable human being,' commented Rodakis, his irony doing little to ease the fury rising inside him.

Anthimos looked at him and said in a grave voice:

'That's right. He is a remarkable human being. He fights for what is good and is willing to sacrifice his own salvation for it. But you don't seem to understand any of that, and you have no idea what you are doing to him.'

'What I am doing to him?' shouted Rodakis, rolling his eyes.

'Of course, if you were willing to be a bit more cooperative, put your ego to one side for a moment, the poor man wouldn't be forced to keep you imprisoned like this, or to bear false witness (which he would do if he had to), or to orchestrate a whole host of deceptions, and burden his soul with sin. He and the rest of us, but the abbot most of all.'

Rodakis took a few steps, his enormous shadow edging its way along the wall.

'Instead of taking advantage of the opportunity the monastery is giving you to put your discovery to proper use, to the benefit of your soul, you choose to barricade yourself inside your selfishness,' Anthimos went on, 'If you were a bit more open-minded, you would see for yourself that your formula should serve a higher purpose. You'd feel so much pride too, knowing that your skill has contributed to the work of Christ, that your discovery really meant something.'

They're stark raving mad, all of them, thought Rodakis in despair.

'But it's not too late to change your mind. Apologise and do the right thing.'

Rodakis lifted the lantern off the floor and went back to his chamber. He was completely at a loss in the face of insanity clothed in the mantle of rationality served up as airtight logic.

'There's something else you don't know.' The words came from behind him; Anthimos was following him.

'What's that?'

'Something that happened a few months ago. Before deciding to summon you, the abbot had tried to use other means to get hold of the information he needed, and was forced on that occasion too to burden his soul with sin.'

Anthimos stopped, as though he had suddenly regretted starting this discussion, as though he had suddenly regretted opening his mouth in the first place. Rodakis picked up on his hesitation.

'Go on. Don't worry. Nothing you can say could lower the abbot in my estimation – what are a few sins between friends, anyway? What did he do?'

'There's a reason why I'm telling you this. He sent someone. One of the brothers…he's no longer with us.'

'Sent him where?' asked Rodakis impatiently, seeing the monk had stopped again.

'Down to your bees. He sent him down there to make a list of all the plants in your garden.'

'How? I had – '

'You'd hired a watchman. I know. A young lad; one of the priest's orphans. Honest, unbribable and what's more, strong. You were there in the mornings and at night it was him, right?'

'Yes, but I don't understand.'

'You don't understand because you don't know, and didn't know then that the young lad had a weakness – now don't start imagining anything – I mean he was a little too fond of the bottle. One night, our brother (and as I said before, he's no longer with us) approached him and talked to him, saying that he had been up all night praying in the wilderness, and the young lad, who'd been brought up to love and respect men of the cloth didn't suspect a thing. The brother produced his hipflask and gave the boy some wine, supposedly a pick-me-up, but he drained the bottle dry, and was soon belting out the words of a rousing hymn in a high-pitched drunken voice. The brother took his chance and vaulted into the garden, but when he saw how much work was involved, he knew that one visit would not be enough. He went back twice: same routine – got the boy drunk and cleared the fence. Even so, he couldn't see much in the dark; let alone distinguish one plant from another. After the third visit, he hadn't managed to record even one third of the plants. But he fully intended to carry on until he had got them all down.'

'So what stopped him from completing this pious task?'

Anthimos pursed his lips and said:

'Death. I told you – he's no longer with us. One morning, as he was collecting water for the plants, a snake bit him. It was fatal, a few hours later he was dead. A horrible viper. We couldn't save him. Such a good lad. It was the old man who took his death the hardest. He took it as a sign. "The signs are crying out – we must not be blind to them; we must heed them," he'd say.'

'So why didn't he heed the signs and give up this absurd project instead of pursuing it so relentlessly?'

'That's where you're mistaken. The abbot did heed the signs. He realised that he would have to find another way of getting the information. He didn't send anybody else down to the garden; but summoned you here instead.'

He went on:

'Look, one man has lost his life. This may have been a punishment for his spying; no other explanation makes sense. Don't you see? Give the abbot what he wants. Stop being so difficult; obey the will of the Lord. It is God's will that the secret formula should pass into the hands of the monastery. I have nothing else to say to you.'

'If that is truly the will of God, then the Almighty will have to come up with a way of getting his hands on it. Because if he's

waiting for me to open my mouth, he's in for a very long wait – from now to eternity.'

Anthimos got up and went back to his corner, unsure whether he had done the right thing. He had disobeyed the abbot's instructions to keep his distance and not to engage the guest in conversation. But the temptation to try had been too great.

After matins the next day, the abbot appeared. Only this time he was very taciturn, his usually animated features strangely impassive. He asked Rodakis if he had reconsidered. When he heard the answer, he simply bent his head and left.

Before acting on his decision to sit down and write to the man who had come looking for Vaya to tell him that he knew where his daughter was, Father Chryssanthos felt it necessary to fill Rosa in on certain facts concerning her background. She was consumed with grief over the man she knew as her father and merely listened impassively as she was told the astonishing truth that he was not after all her father, and was not even a distant relative. All she wanted was for him to be found and come home.

But when the priest told her that her real father lived in a far off corner of the country, a faint spark of interest appeared in her eyes. He said that he could not give her an opinion on the man as he had only spoken to him very briefly, but stressed that nothing could alter the fact that it was he who had given her life. Rosa was not against the idea of meeting her new father or even moving near him, maybe – one day.

After a while Father Chryssanthos wrote to make the necessary arrangements, and, having satisfied himself that Rodakis's house was properly locked up, boarded the ship with Rosa one stormy day and set off for the town where Stefanos T. lived.

The town did not worry her. She was used to it from the many occasions Rodakis had taken her with him to get supplies. The busy streets, people stopping to talk to each other, the shops, and most of all, the huge market – fruit, dead poultry and big barrels of salted fish – filled her with the joy of living. The priest, concentrating more on Rosa than on the street signs (which they would pay for by going round and round in circles), noted this lightness in her mood and took it as confirmation that he was doing the right thing.

Stefanos T.'s house was in the centre of the city. Before they knocked, Father Chryssanthos crossed himself and in a shaky, breathless voice, brought on as much by the emotion of the moment as by all the walking they'd done, announced to Rosa that a new chapter in her life was about to begin. She returned his solemn look, and made him swear that if Rodakis were ever found alive, he would come and fetch her. The priest didn't swear, but he gave his word, and knocked on the door. A few ponderous but hurried movements were heard from inside before an elderly man with white hair opened the door. He looked at the girl standing on his doorstep for a few moments, his eyes swollen with tears, and pulled her into a tight embrace before falling to his knees and smothering the priest's hand with kisses of gratitude.

They went up to the first floor. Rosa did not take her eyes off Stefanos T. for a moment. She was astonished to see how old he was. The two men steered clear of the thornier issues in the story, so no mention was made of either Vaya or Rodakis. They chatted about the island, comparing life there with life in the city as well as various other anodyne topics. But harmless though their small talk was, it couldn't stop Stefanos T. from periodically wiping the tears from his eyes. Rosa suddenly piped up and asked him why he had kept himself hidden away all these years and why she had grown up thinking another man was her father. The priest, who until that moment had made a point of not going into detail, hurriedly answered in a voice designed to discourage her from asking any more questions. He explained that in life there are certain situations best left in God's hands and in God's hands alone.

A middle-aged woman, Stefanos T.'s housekeeper, walked in to serve iced water and fruit, and later showed Rosa and the priest to their rooms. Father Chryssanthos had decided to stay on a couple of days to see Rosa settled in. She was given a box-shaped room with a window looking out onto a three-sided piazza. It led into another room, but the communicating door was locked and a large table, a sort of desk, was pushed up against it with a porcelain statue of the Virgin Mary standing on it, her arms folded across her chest across her and her gaze lowered.

She liked her bed with its thick mattress and its three puffy pillows, and she liked the ceiling with its garlanded plaster cornices, and was glad that she had come to live somewhere new and had got away from the old house which was haunted by memories of her vanished parents. The only thing she didn't much care for was the fact that her new father was so old.

When he left, the priest promised that he would come back to visit her in a fortnight to see if all was well with her and her new family. He bent over and whispered confidentially in her ear that she should really make an effort to establish a warm relationship with her father. She nodded, as though giving her word.

Stefanos T. was walking on air. He did everything he could to please his daughter, his only child. He showed her all the nicest parts of the city, and gave her treats and new experiences: meals in restaurants serving dishes with foreign names and exotic fruit; walks in the big parks and outings to the zoo; trips to the theatre and visits to his friends' houses. Rosa's mere existence – her beauty and spontaneity were ample reward for Stefanos T.

Therefore, when, true to his word, Father Chryssanthos returned two weeks later, he was delighted and relieved to see the two people he had brought together so happy. Rosa, radiant in her new clothes, struggled to describe all the new worlds that had opened up for her. At some point, Stefanos T. took the priest to one side and told him that he had contacted a lawyer to handle the business of paternity; in the event that he could not establish paternity, he was determined to adopt Rosa so that one day she could inherit his property.

'I approve wholeheartedly,' said the priest, thinking his mission had reached a satisfactory conclusion. When he left, he said that his next visit would be shortly before the holidays, about two months away.

'Try to love him – he's a good man,' he whispered to Rosa as they said their farewells.

That evening after supper, just like all the evenings when nothing in particular had been planned, Stefanos T. retired to his favourite armchair where he would sit for a long time, semi-dozing, before deciding to transfer to a proper bed. Rosa meanwhile would attend to some small chores, or chat with the housekeeper. Before taking herself off to bed, she would tip-toe into the sitting room and say good night to her father. That night was no different.

It didn't take more than the slightest creak of the hinges to wake Stefanos T. – that sweet sound he waited for so eagerly, even in his sleep. Rosa walked over to him to say goodnight. He held out his hand and stroked her hair fondly, just as he did every night before she went off to bed. But that night, Rosa did not go off to bed. She stood there, staring at her father's bushy eyebrows. He took this as a sign that she wanted to say something, and gave her an encouraging smile.

'Father,' she said softly, 'I want you to know that I love you.'

Overwhelmed by emotion, he struggled to fight back the tears, and smiled at her again, this time in gratitude.

Rosa sat down on his lap, just as she used to sit on Rodakis's knee. She moved her face up and let her cheek fall onto his. Stefanos T. welcomed this display of affection. Then she pressed her mouth against the deep wrinkle scored into his cheek, slowly moving her lips until they met his, puckered and pushed her tongue through while her hands sought out Stefanos T.'s ageing chest. The effect of all this on the old man was instant – like an intravenous poison shooting through his veins, leaving him in a state of immediate paralysis. Rosa climbed off his lap and kneeling down on the floor started rubbing her face against his knees, which automatically tensed up in self-defence. She brought her head up higher until she found the soft swelling she was looking for.

It was not until then that Stefanos T. regained control over his muscles. He grabbed her by the arms, and with as much force as he could muster, threw her off. A mixture of loathing and horror immediately erased all the other feelings he might have had for the bemused creature looking up at him from where she had fallen to the floor.

'Go to your room at once,' he croaked, unable to say anything more.

Rosa got to her feet, her body aching from the fall, opened the sitting room door and went to her room. She wanted to cry. That her affection should be returned with such violence was beyond her comprehension.

Sitting down on the edge of her bed, she called up the image of Rodakis. Not that she had ever stopped thinking about him, but at that moment she needed him terribly. She remembered how much he used to enjoy her caresses, how he would close his eyes and abandon himself to her little displays of tenderness, and how afterwards, when her tiny hands were tired after all that stroking and massaging, he would kiss her affectionately on the face and neck. She remembered how he would snap her breasts between his teeth, pretending to be a wild dog, and how his pretend barking would send her into fits of giggles. He never hurt her – he knew exactly how much pressure to apply with his jaws, just enough to reach but never cross the threshold of pain. And then she remembered his tongue, warm inside her belly button, on her thighs, along her hip bone.

Tears rolled down her face. Stefanos T.'s sudden harshness hurt her deeply, particularly as it came at a time when she was trying her best to do what the priest had told her to do: overlook his advanced years, turn a blind eye to his scrawny old body, his empty gums and his bald head.

'He might be one of those people who just don't like being touched,' she reasoned in an attempt to make excuses for him, and derived a degree of comfort from this thought.

She wiped the tears off her cheek, and felt her face cool down. Then she forced herself to go to sleep, soothing herself with memories of the afternoons when she used to doze off in Rodakis's arms, her nose buried in his armpit, inhaling the delicate, slightly bitter smell of his body.

Rosa recovered fairly easily from that evening's traumatic episode. The same could not be said for Stefanos T.

The disillusionment, the destruction of a dream: all those years chasing the dream, the dream finally coming true, only to turn into the worst kind of nightmare. Who could have imagined that such a horrific thing could have happened to him in the twilight of his days. He regretted having started his desperate search for the child; he wished he had never disembarked on that accursed island; had never set eyes on that priest; had never received his letter. But he could not turn the clock back now; the only thing left to do was to concentrate on the future.

As soon as he heard Rosa close her bedroom door behind her, he stood up and called the housekeeper. The woman, who was getting ready for bed, shocked by the sense of emergency she heard in his voice, came running without delay, dressed though she was in her nightgown. Looking like a startled magpie, her eyes bulging with curiosity, she asked him what the matter was.

'The girl is sick, I'm sorry to say,' answered Stefanos T. 'She's got the same thing her mother had: the same tainted genes.'

'Is it serious?' asked the housekeeper, clearly concerned.

'Listen,' said Stefanos T. squeezing her wrist, 'this conversation stays within these walls. Is that understood?'

Her silence was guaranteed. He continued:

'She's got the devil inside her. She's a nymphomaniac.'

He struggled to get the words out.

'She wants a man – any male she can get her hands on.'

'Our little girl?' asked the housekeeper, dumbfounded. 'Our little Rosa?'

'I don't know what it was like on the island. People who live close to nature often give their instincts freer rein; it makes me sick to think of how many fishermen and shepherds have had their way with her. Looks like she started to feel a bit restricted here, and when she couldn't contain her lust any longer…she turned her attentions on me…'

'What do you mean? Whatever do you mean?'

'Exactly what I said. Don't make me this any harder for me than it already is.'

'I can't believe what I'm hearing. Are you sure there hasn't been some terrible misunderstanding?'

Stefanos T. shook his head in sadness.

She tried again:

'Perhaps you got the wrong end of the stick.'

'Look – I know what's what, I can tell a kiss and a caress when I see one, woman. What I don't know is how to deal with this situation.'

'What can you do? If all this is true, there isn't anything anyone can do. Not the doctor. Not anybody.'

'What if I can't cure her? We have to nip this in the bud. I want you to listen and listen carefully. Rule No.1: From now on she is not to leave the house alone – it would be like sending a lamb into the wolf's lair. The first passer-by might lead her astray. Is that clear?'

'She never goes anywhere alone anyway. She always comes with me, to the shops or…except…'

'What?'

'When I send her on errands, here in the neighbourhood. But she never takes long. She's there and back before you know it.'

'Don't send her out again. I want her supervised at all times.'

'Fine.'

'And from now on, I want the front door to be kept locked, whether you are in the house or not. And she is not to go out unless she's with you.'

The housekeeper let out a deep sigh.

'I can't get over it. That innocent child. When did all this happen?'

'My orders are to take effect immediately. Right away. Go down and lock up.' His voice suddenly cracked and tears leapt out from his eyes.

'You poor thing, you poor suffering thing,' said the woman, drawing his head into her bosom and squeezing it.

Stefanos T. sank gratefully into the warmth of her ample breasts, so familiar to him from their sexual intimacies of the past, and let his warm tears spill onto them.

'I'll watch out for her, don't you worry, my dear. You'll see; we'll find a good man to marry her and she'll calm down, slake her thirst. Everything will be fine.'

'Go on – go and lock the door, please.'

The housekeeper got up from the arm of the chair where she'd been perching while Stefanos T.'s head had been nestling in her bosom, and went down to lock the door.

As he heard her footsteps going down the staircase it occurred to him that he should shout down to her to lock the kitchen door that led into the garden via the fire escape. But instead of her name, he heard himself emit a distorted, incoherent wail, or rather a shriek. His jaw, suddenly uncoordinated and slack, slipped impotently to one side while his tongue, now unnaturally flaccid, tried in vain to approximate some consonants. However, the sound he made was sufficiently audible and penetrating to have the housekeeper rushing back upstairs without locking up. When she saw Stefanos T. still in his armchair, waving his hand around in a bizarre manner, his madly automated eyebrows dancing up and down, she thought she had better go and fetch the doctor.

On very bright days, when the sun's rays were refracted through the light shaft of the Error Room, Rodakis would examine the surface of each wall in detail. By scrutinising the marks left by the iron tools, he tried to speculate on the mood and thoughts of the monks as they attacked the hard surfaces. The painstaking care and skill applied to the walls were evident from the fine vertical lines achieved by precise, controlled hammering; perhaps each line had been executed with a prayer, like beads on a rosary. But there were areas where Rodakis's eye caught the small, almost imperceptible depressions caused by overzealous banging; he suspected that they might have been the effect of a bad mood, the result of some unpleasant incident or indisposition which had made the monk in question careless and distracted. There were not many, and careful inspection of the walls yielded the conclusion that whoever had been responsible for this room had worked with a clear mind and a calm spirit, and had thrown themselves body and soul into the task.

It was harder to draw conclusions about the adjoining cell because it was always so dark, even on the brightest days. Nevertheless, the difference was obvious. The impression given by the dark cell was that it had been completed in a hurry, with very little concern for aesthetics. The walls were not even straight; they seemed to slope at a peculiar angle and the surfaces were rough, full of pockmarks of various sizes. Rodakis guessed that the monk working here had brought little enthusiasm to it, and had performed his task out of duty, reluctant to go against the general ethos of the monastery. Then again, it was conceivable that the exact opposite was true – that he had thrown himself into it with great gusto but with a passion that was not conducive to careful and conscientious work. If the latter were true, he should have pulled himself together to ensure a perfect result, unless he had been distracted by something along the way, something that had dampened his enthusiasm – such as the tragic error which led to the joining of the two cells. Could that be why the inner cell had been left half-finished? Nobody knew the answer.

Many hours were devoted to the study of the walls. This was his strategy for dealing with his worst enemies – inertia and inactivity. Not loneliness; he'd been used to that for years. This routine of inch for inch inspection and speculation helped keep his mind active and stable. The low points were those terrible winter evenings when he was forced to slide the wooden cover over the light shaft and make do with the wan lamplight and the hazy glow from the brazier the abbot had been kind enough to provide.

Rodakis had been incarcerated in the Error Room for five and a half months now. Anthimos was no longer with him round the clock but looked in on him every day and brought him food. When Rodakis asked him when the abbot was intending to come, Anthimos always replied that it would depend on when he was ready to share his secret; otherwise there was nothing to discuss. If Rodakis needed anything, he, Anthimos, would take care of it – which was after all the reason for his daily visits to the cell.

One day the prisoner asked for a pen and a piece of paper. Anthimos was quick to oblige. He handed over the writing equipment and was asked to wait outside. After approximately one hour, Rodakis called him back, saying that he had written out the formula, and would hand it over as soon as he was released. Anthimos, hearing this, rushed off.

He reckoned that the abbot would soon make an appearance, but nothing happened for several hours. He entered the cell with Anthimos from the door of the dark cell and stood at the point where the two cells divided, white as a ghost with a look of frosty displeasure on his face, as though he had been dragged down there against his will.

'Very well, Rodakis: I'm listening.'

He lifted up the piece of paper.

'I'm ready,' he said. 'Let me out of here and the formula is yours.'

'Don't worry,' said the abbot, 'as soon as you give us what we want, we won't have any reason to keep you here. Personally, I will be very happy to see you leave this appalling cell and return to your old life back home with your daughter. Just tell us your secret, and everything will return to normal.'

Rodakis looked him straight in the eye and extended the hand holding the paper.

'Here you are. I trust you. Take it.'

The abbot approached him, extending his own hand; the crunch of his shoulder joint piercing the silence. His bony fingers snatched the sheet of paper out of Rodakis's hand and without so much as glancing at it, he crumpled it up in his palm, squeezed it into a ball and tossed it onto the brazier. A stifled cry of disappointment came from behind him; Anthimos had been watching in secret.

'It seems that you have yet to understand the will of the Lord: what He wants and what He expects from you. When you are sincere, and have abandoned these absurd tricks, which do neither of us justice, I'll be waiting.' He turned and left the cell.

With this last sentence, the flaming tongue, which all the time had projected a flickering, shadowy light across the abbot's cheek, gobbled up the crumpled paper ball and died, so abruptly and completely as to suggest that the length of the abbot's speech had been deliberately synchronised with the duration of the flame.

Rodakis was alone again. How had the abbot known that he had not written down the proper recipe? Had he been expecting it? Even if he had suspected that Rodakis would not part with the formula so readily and might try to dupe him, surely he wouldn't have tossed the sheet of paper into the fire without the slightest hesitation. It occurred to Rodakis that the abbot might have been putting him to the test: he had not made the slightest protest when challenged, which was tantamount to an admission of guilt. The abbot knew very well that if the recipe were genuine, all he would have to do was to ask Rodakis to rewrite it. He concluded that had he been quick enough to react more wisely and more calmly, he would be a free man now.

Without wasting another moment, he took a fresh sheet of paper and wrote out the formula again, with a number of alterations. He knocked loudly on the iron door. This proved effective: a monk, possibly one that had been working on the construction of the dome, appeared and asked why he was hitting the door in this maniacal fashion.

'The abbot. Tell the abbot I want to see him. Tell him I'm sorry and this time there will be no tricks,' he shouted.

A few hours later, in place of the abbot, Anthimos appeared. With a deprecating look on his face he announced that the abbot was in no mood to be deceived, and did not see the point of going all the way down there just to toss another useless scrap of paper onto the fire. Despite Rodakis's protestations that this time he had written down the real formula, and his warning that they were pushing their luck, Anthimos would not be turned. Impervious to all the entreaties pursuing him through the barred door to the Error Room, he left.

Between then and the following spring, Rodakis made a further two attempts to fool the abbot, sending word through Anthimos that he was ready to reveal the secret formula. But the abbot didn't even go to the trouble of getting angry: he merely sent word back via Anthimos that the time would come when the divine formula would be his. Rodakis was feeling increasingly ensnared and could see no way out. He began to wonder whether he would ever be free again, whether he was destined to end his days buried deep inside the stony belly of the Site. A new fear started to torment him: what if he did decide to hand over the true formula and, after all these tricks, could not convince them that he was telling the truth – would he stay locked up until the Second Coming? Perhaps the abbot really was in possession of an infallible instinct, which could reliably alert him when people were lying and when they were telling the truth.

He picked up his last blank sheet of paper and started to write out the real formula – the exact combination of plants that resulted in Angelico. When Anthimos brought him his food later that evening, Rodakis told him once again that he needed to see the abbot so that he could pass on the details of his discovery. Anthimos shook his head, patently unconvinced. 'I'll tell him when I see him,' he said, unenthusiastically, adding, 'If I remember, that is.'

'Make sure you do.'

Anthimos had heard all this before. He locked the door and left. By some coincidence, he bumped into the abbot as soon as he emerged from through outside gate. He conveyed the message. As he repeated the words of his exchange with the prisoner, the abbot turned paler and paler and suddenly strode off, disappearing into the dark hole in the hillside so quickly that he looked more like a haystack swept along by the current than a human being.

The key turned impatiently. From the manner in which the abbot entered the cell, out of breath, dishevelled, his eyes watering from the perspiration dripping into them, Rodakis thought that he was in the presence of some strange mythological creature straight from the pages of his childhood storybooks.

'What do you want?' he asked the old man, startled, as though he had not been the one to ask for him only a few minutes earlier, as though this visit was a complete surprise.

'Anthimos said – give it to me...'

His voice was shaky.

He took a step closer to him. He saw the paper in his hand.

'Give me, the...'

Rodakis pulled back. He had no intention of handing over his secret. The abbot came even closer. He stretched out his hand and would definitely have reached Rodakis if the prisoner had not darted into the adjoining cell.

The abbot pursued him. His crooked fingers grasped Rodakis's shoulder, causing it to go numb and relax its grip on the paper. The abbot made a grab for it, but Rodakis blocked his path. A struggle followed, each using his body to fend off the other. Anthimos, who had followed the abbot down, stood by and watched, debating on whether he should intervene, until he heard his name issuing from the old man's tensed jaw.

In two long strides he reached the struggling bodies. The fight would have been over if Rodakis had not managed to undo his trousers and urinate all over the carefully penned formula. Anthimos seized him by the collar and sent him flying into the corner while the abbot got down on his knees and snatched up the paper, which was quickly absorbing the liquid. He opened his eyes wide to read it – as though all the information in it could be digested and retained in a single reading, even if it were possible to stop the liquid eating into the ink and blurring the delicately formed letters until they all merged together into one unique, shapeless stain of diluted ink.

Towards the end of the spring a significant change occurred. The doors of the Error Room were opened and he now had the freedom, not, of course to go out, but to move freely within the confines of the stone edifice for a few hours each day, usually a few hours in the afternoon until it got dark. The metal entrance door naturally remained locked at all times. This was a gesture of goodwill on the part of the abbot, but was nevertheless inauspicious, carrying a suggestion that his stay inside the Site was expected to be long term, hence the decision to allow him a little extra comfort.

While he roamed the dark corridors, there was no one with him and he was given the run of the place (with the exception of certain rooms that were permanently sealed off). The first time he left his cell he discovered to his disappointment that it was not just the metal door that barred the exit; there was another door he didn't remember seeing which isolated the second room (the one the anchorite had opened) from the rest of the structure. This door deprived him of his only contact with the outside, albeit through iron bars. There was no way out of the Site.

During his wanderings through the irregular passage-ways, he would often cross paths with various brothers who routinely ignored him as though he were invisible; they were probably under strict instructions to do so. Rodakis assumed that these monks were either going to or leaving the dome where everybody worked in shifts. In the dim light, with the uniform cassocks and beards, it was hard for him to distinguish individuals; only a few prominent features stood out – the odd pair of deep blue eyes, an enormous, aquiline nose, that familiar bulging forehead, a wart sprouting in the gap between the eyebrows – that was all that stood out in his memory.

One day on his way back to his cell, he was climbing a small flight of steps at the beginning of the diagonal passage leading to the Error Room, when he crossed paths with a monk who was hurrying down. The only thing about the monk he could see was his cassock sleeve, and he caught the draught from it straight on his cheek as it flapped up. When he mounted the last step, a vague force stopped him in his tracks and made him turn round to look at the monk who had also stopped and was looking back up the stairs.

He instantly recognised Paschalis's piercing eyes, cloaked in the pale oval hood which left his hair and beard exposed, crossing the small distance that stood between them. This was the second time he had seen him (curiously, the first time was also on a staircase, when he saw him at work on the dome), and now he was convinced that it was his former assistant. Then it occurred to him that Paschalis might be in some way connected with his incarceration, and his mind raced to find what that connection could be.

'So you're here too.'

'I've been here much longer than you have,' replied Paschalis.

'Any idea why I'm here?'

'Of course I do. Everybody knows why you're here.'

'What is your opinion of all this?'

'My opinion?'

'Yes. Don't you agree that I am the victim of a terrible injustice?'

'Life is full of injustices. There's nothing new about that. It's only when we are the victims that they seem so terrible to us.'

His words betrayed a note of bitterness and Rodakis wondered whether what had taken place between the two of them in the past might be to blame. This thought tallied with his earlier speculations.

'How's your sister?'

'I don't know. I never hear from her. Her land, I don't know if you remember...'

'Of course I remember. What happened?'

'She lost it.'

'I hope you don't bear me any grudges; I know you held me responsible back then for all the ills befalling you and your family.'

'No, not at all. After all, you've paid for your mistakes – you're still paying for them. Quite heavily: losing your wife; being separated from your daughter; imprisoned. The way I see it, that whole business with the honey has brought you more suffering than joy.'

'And this pleases you, no doubt?'

Paschalis was temporarily silenced by this, and stood there like a pillar of salt.

'I try not to let it. I tell myself not to enjoy it. Sometimes I feel sorry for you, sometimes I don't. I'm not a saint, you know.'

Rodakis walked down two steps, and in a perceptibly louder voice, asked Paschalis a question, which, caught in echo by the rock, intensified and multiplied.

'What's your part in all this?' he asked pointing to the stone shell surrounding them.

Paschalis's expression darkened and his eyes glazed over as though he had taken refuge behind a fine, invisible film.

'You think that I had something to do with your imprisonment here?'

'Precisely.'

'Of course I do.'

His eyes came to life again.

'Since you're so curious, you might as well know that I'm the reason you're here. I approached the old man about Angelico, got hold of some for him to taste. I was largely responsible for giving him the idea we needed to own it. I went with him to those remote villages to try it out on the peasants, telling them it was honey from holy soil. He told you about that. After that, everything was the abbot's initiative. Nothing to do with me.'

'I see your revenge was plotted very carefully. I obviously underestimated you.'

Paschalis received the insult with equanimity; there was no sign of his formerly explosive ego; no protest, no need to repay the slight. All he did was bend his head, deep in thought.

'It wasn't revenge,' he said. 'That time when you came and told me you were giving up building work to throw yourself into an experiment, or something of that kind, and I realised that it meant I would be out of work at a time when I desperately needed money. I hated you. I won't pretend I didn't. But when I spoke to the abbot about Angelico, I wasn't doing it to get back at you. More than ten years had passed. But deep down inside, I felt that I'd had a hand in the development of Angelico; I had made a sacrifice, and I wanted to see that sacrifice bear fruit. I wanted to be able to say to myself that everything I'd suffered on account of your wretched experiment had helped a lot of people and didn't just fatten your wallet. As for revenge, well, I got a lot of satisfaction back then from beating you to a pulp; at the time I didn't understand what was driving me to hit you – it was like I wasn't in control of my fists. I can still remember the feeling.'

'That day,' said Rodakis, 'you did not let me, I didn't manage to tell you, I had been thinking about your situation. Just as I was going to tell you what I had in mind for you, you went for me, and I found myself on my back, on the ground. I had been intending to help you. I wasn't about to leave you like that – at least until you found another job. I was going to give you money, you imbecile. That same day. Do you see how differently things would have turned out if you hadn't been in such a hurry to demonstrate how tough you are? Your sister, you, me – we'd all be sitting happily at home now.'

'I was going to enter the monastery anyway. As for the rest...'

He tried to digest what he had heard and imagine the turn things probably would have taken. But his expression immediately changed, taking on an air of insolence that reminded Rodakis of the good old days.

'How do I know you're telling the truth?'

Rodakis realised that there was little sense in prolonging their conversation. He turned, and after taking his leave of Paschalis said:

'Your stupidity is astounding.'

He entered his cell, trying not to allow this encounter to bother him, even though it made the sequence of events leading up to his confinement much clearer.

His back, which had been bothering him since the morning, was still causing him discomfort. He was sure that the damp was responsible, especially at night when he could feel it penetrate his skin and gnaw away at his bones. He also felt it was the cause of various other changes he'd been noticing recently, such as the stiffening in his knee, and the shooting pain in his elbows and shoulders, which were becoming increasingly frequent.

'It's to be expected – humans were not made for subterranean living,' he said to himself.

He closed his eyes but sleep did not come as his mind started to work on this question: Was he underground? To somebody walking around on the hill it might seem that he was; but if somebody was standing at the foot of the hill and had to look up in order to discern the top, they would either agree that he was underground or would realise that he was actually higher than the observer himself, and therefore more elevated than the ground he was walking on, not underground at all but simply inside the ground. The further Rodakis progressed down the tunnel of sleep, the more impossible the question of whether there was a distinction between underground and in the ground became.

The three-sided piazza was empty. It was always empty at this time. After a while, a man appeared. He was short. He sat down on one of the three benches, his eyes fixed in one direction. A tall woman suddenly arrived; she came from the direction he'd been looking in. She was much taller than he was. She sat down next to him; they greeted each other. Nothing else was said, as they sat there, looking in different directions as though they were strangers, coincidentally enjoying the peace of the deserted piazza. Then the tall woman, completely without warning, launched into an interminable monologue punctuated with neurotic gestures and grimaces distorting her features. All this was directed at the man, who simply sat and listened, making no attempt to interrupt her. Just as suddenly as she had begun, she dried up, and the piazza sank back into silence. At some point, the man stood up, walked around the bench and sat down again. He turned to face the woman and abandoning his muteness, he started yelling at the top of his lungs, pounding the bench with his fist while his face turned from puce to red. He paused when a small child with a brightly coloured flag passed by and resumed as soon as it was out of sight. The woman turned her back on him, pretending to look at the sky. This provoked him further; he shot to his feet and stood over her, but she simply covered her ears and started swinging her legs in time to an imaginary upbeat tune. By now out of control, he started to whack his thighs with his clenched fists and moved to another bench. She unplugged her ears, smoothed down her clothes, and left in the same direction she had come from, followed from a distance of a few metres by the short man. Then they disappeared from Rosa's field of vision.

This was just one scene of the many she observed every day from her bedroom window. The fact that she was unable to hear the lines her protagonists exchanged did not detract from her enjoyment. To some extent, it actually contributed to the interest as she was required to write these inaudible dialogues from imagination and to create each character and incident. Besides, there was little else to do; it was hard to fill her time, permanently locked up in her bedroom as she was.

After the shock Stefanos T. had undergone, his house-keeper concluded that the surest way to carry out his wishes that Rosa should not be exposed to the dangers of the male sex was to keep her locked up in her bedroom. This also relieved her of the constant anxiety over whether the door was locked or not, and that Rosa would somehow find a way to get out. In an effort to make the room more comfortable for the girl, she pulled the table that blocked the door to the adjoining room and opened up the other room for her, giving her two rooms instead of one, only the second room didn't have a window and had probably been intended as a storeroom more than a bedroom.

'These are your father's wishes, your sick father's wishes,' Rosa was informed, 'so he can be sure that nothing will happen to you now that he cannot keep an eye on you himself.'

She was reassured that if she needed anything, all she needed to do was knock on the door, and she would come right away.

Rosa acquiesced; if that was what her father wanted, she would obey. But she thought of Rodakis, who would never have come up with such an insane idea.

She visited Stefanos T. once a day, at a time chosen by the housekeeper. She would sit on the edge of the bed and look at him in silence, thinking that if he was unable to speak, she had better not either. The housekeeper was always present during these mute visits, standing silently in the corner. Sometimes he would simply look at her from deep within a vacant serenity and on other occasions, he would lash out in small fits of violence the moment she entered the room, lifting his head, snarling and clutching the edge of his blanket with his fists; or his body would go into a series of convulsions which would often send him onto the floor. At first this terrified Rosa and made her want to cry, but after a while she became accustomed to these bizarre outbursts. She also noted that the less flustered she became, they sooner they were over.

The old man's condition neither deteriorated nor improved. The doctor said that there was no immediate threat to his health; but on the other hand, there was no sign of recovery. After her brief visits to her father, Rosa would return to her room, the housekeeper locking the door behind her. The first thing she did was to go into the dark room and pray with all her heart for her father's recovery. Then she'd move up to the window. And then bed. She slept a lot: ten, twelve, fourteen hours a day. On waking, she'd take up her position by the window again, and as time went by, she grew increasingly accustomed to this new routine. Eventually, her incarceration no longer bothered her. She had never really enjoyed much freedom anyway; she had been raised within the limits of the property, and as a baby she had spent an inordinate amount of time locked up inside a trunk. She was fond of her two rooms, and looked on them as some kind of extension of her self, in much the same way as a tortoise regards its shell. She was ruled by the belief that so long as these walls remained in place, solid and untouched, she really had nothing to fear at all.

At twilight she was frequently overcome by feelings of sadness and melancholy – in her view inexplicable, as she had everything a human being could wish for: a roof over her head; food on her plate; and life in the bosom of her family. Never mind that this family consisted of a sick old man and a housekeeper (who without being overly affectionate, was always polite to her). When she went to bed still carrying this indefinable sadness within her, she would think of her mother, and the time when they used to sleep together in the same bedroom. She remembered when she was little, how every time she was sad or afraid and couldn't get to sleep, she would hear Vaya – who had been asleep for hours – talking to herself, tossing and turning in terror, as though the child's sadness had transferred itself to her and disturbed her sleep.

These memories intensified her sadness. Now there was nobody there to talk in their sleep when she felt miserable at night.

'Rodakis, I've got something here I'm sure you'll want to see,' said Anthimos, hurtling into the Error Room like a whirlwind, with an expression that was a patent betrayal of his intention to pique Rodakis's curiosity.

The fact that he had been foregoing his daily walk recently and would sit in silence in his cell all day, clearly in bad humour, gave rise to concerns over his health, specifically his state of mind. Anthimos, noticing that Rodakis was looking drawn – a sure sign of weight loss – alerted the abbot who put it down to nostalgia for his old life, which could be interpreted as a sign of health, and might lead him to break his silence over the formula. Nevertheless, he instructed Anthimos to do his best to lift Rodakis's spirits.

'Oh? And what's that?' replied Rodakis, listlessly, belying the curiosity in his eyes.

He was not holding anything and judging by the movements

as he sat down next to him on the straw mattress, whatever it was must have been concealed high up in his cassock sleeve. He rested his gaze on that spot and waited. Anthimos duly inserted his hand into his sleeve where it disappeared and emerged, holding up a book, which was promptly deposited into Rodakis's lap. Rodakis looked at it and froze. After the initial shock, he picked it up.

'This is just like a book I bought years ago. It was devoured by a dog; I had been foolish enough to lend it to somebody.'

'It's not "just like" the one you bought. It is the one you bought,' said Anthimos. 'The one you lent to your sister. She brought it here herself.'

'She sold it,' said Rodakis in a half-whisper, his upper lip forming a curl as his forefinger traced the tooled outline of the apple tree.

'No, she didn't sell it. Not really. She brought it to the abbot as a gift to soften him up over some business with her husband. I was present at the time. She said it was the only thing of value she had and thought it would bring pleasure to someone like the old man. She said you'd brought it back for her from some trip, I think – not that she'd borrowed it from you. The old man took it and did her the favour she wanted. He said it was a wonderful book, and I thought you might like to see it again. So you lent it to her, did you? You didn't give it to her?'

Rodakis did not answer.

'Well, if that's the case, strictly speaking, the book belongs to you. But let the old man decide that,' he added hastily.

'I never thought I'd see it again,' he said, turning a few pages, the colour returning to his face.

Anthimos's action brought the desired result. Later that day Rodakis not only decided to take his constitutional but also inquired about the progress of the dome and asked if he might see it. The monks who were working at the time told him that the tunnelling wouldn't take much longer, but even after that there would be a lot of work to do; the opening of the large light shaft through the centre of the roof was going to be particularly awkward as they were unable to calculate with any accuracy the distance between them and ground level. They were considering boring some exploratory holes from the outside of the structure from the top of the hill.

Rodakis found the atmosphere inside stifling, and had difficulty breathing; he wondered how anyone could work in such conditions. For a moment, as he looked at those five monks bent over in the lamplight, chisels in hand, hacking away tirelessly at the last section of the hill, he felt a shudder run through him. The figures looked like something straight out of a nightmare – frozen in time, condemned to everlasting penal servitude.

T. Rosenmann's long voyage over calm waters brought him to the island on the day of the summer equinox. In his pocket was the map he'd been sold two years earlier by the pushy character down at the harbour. This time he had an interpreter in tow, a short fellow with a ginger goatee. It had not been easy to find the right person for the job: someone proficient in the language, available for travel, and whose company was tolerable.

They arrived several hours before nightfall, but T. Rosenmann was unable to decide whether it was wise to try to visit Rodakis immediately or wait until the following day. He decided to wait, despite his impatience for the meeting, reasoning that it would be better not to rush into anything without first working out a strategy. The two men rented some rooms above a coffee house.

The following morning, T. Rosenmann found it impossible to wake his interpreter who was peeved to learn that his duties involved a walk of several hours; he eventually relented when he heard that he would be remunerated for his pains. Even so, they got off to a slow start as the interpreter refused to leave the room without shaving, a process that proved painfully slow.

In every other respect, the walk through the varied landscape of the island was uneventful as T. Rosenmann more or less remembered the way. His interpreter turned out to be capable of very engaging conversation, so he relaxed and, apart from the nausea brought on whenever he found himself downstream of the man's unfortunate choice of cologne, enjoyed himself. They arrived shortly before midday.

'I don't think anybody's around,' said the interpreter, who had been expecting to find long queues of people outside the house.

'No. How strange; they could be out on errands, or working somewhere else for the season.'

The disappointment shattered his expectations, but his voice quickly recovered its usual steadiness.

'But look – they're not away. Our people are here all right. I saw somebody tweaking the curtain in the upstairs window. Don't look! Let's knock.'

They stood there for some time, but it was not until they knocked for a second time that footsteps could be heard on the other side of the door. But nobody opened the door. The interpreter took the initiative of knocking for a third time. The door opened instantly. It was as though the person behind it had suddenly decided to put their hesitations aside and confront their uninvited guests head on.

The puzzled face of a woman appeared in the opening between the door and the frame. The interpreter said that they had come to see Rodakis and added, again on his own initiative, that they were there on very urgent business and would not leave until they had spoken to him. The woman pulled back the door a little wider, and with even greater astonishment than before, announced:

'My brother is not here. It's been a year since – Who are you?'

'The gentleman here is from abroad and I am his interpreter. We wish to see Mr Rodakis on a very important matter. We are confident that he will be interested in our proposal…did you say he was your brother? Mr Rodakis is your brother?'

'My brother. That's right.'

'You say that he is away?'

'My brother, Sir… We lost him a year ago.'

'I beg your pardon!'

'What's going on? Who is this lady?' asked T. Rosenmann, who until then had been standing there in passive incomprehension.

'She is his sister. She says that her brother is dead.'

'Dead? When?'

'A year ago, she says.'

'That's terrible,' muttered T. Rosenmann.

'Our deepest condolences, Madam,' said the interpreter, possibly a little too emphatically.

'We're not sure that he's dead. I mean, we don't really know.'

'But didn't you just say that you had lost him a year ago?'

'Yes, I did. We lost him. What I mean is, he disappeared. But his body's never been found. He's never been found: dead or alive.'

'He disappeared?'

'Off the face of the earth.'

'What did he die of?' T. Rosenmann asked.

'It's not clear that he did.'

'What?'

'Please come inside,' said E. Rodakis, opening the door even further.

The interpreter signalled to T. Rosenmann to follow her and at the same time said:

'He vanished without trace. Nobody knows if he's alive or dead.'

'Perhaps he's been kidnapped – ask her – someone who wanted to make use of his expertise.'

She took them into the big room.

'Have you considered the possibility that he's been kidnapped by somebody who needed his expertise? You know what I'm referring to.'

'Angelico?'

T. Rosenmann's eyes lit up at the sound of that name.

'What can I say? I can't believe something like that could have happened.'

'Have you asked her yet?'

'She thinks it highly unlikely.'

'Pity. All my plans have been blown sky high.'

'Is there anything else you want me to ask her?'

'Yes. Ask her – although it's too much to hope for – ask her if her brother ever confided his secret formula in her or anyone else.'

The interpreter communicated the question.

'Good heavens! If I knew that I would be a very wealthy woman. Anyway, even if I did, I would never admit it, let alone share it with you – if you'll excuse my bluntness.'

'What did she say?'

'Just a moment,' cut in the interpreter as though annoyed by the interruption, and turned immediately back to E. Rodakis. 'If you were in possession of the formula, the gentleman here would offer you exactly what he came to offer your brother. A very interesting and…generous offer.'

'My brother, gentlemen, my brother – God rest his soul if he is in fact dead – was a man who is hard to describe. He never functioned like other people. That's why we never got on, even though he was very fond of me. It's understandable that you thought that he might have told me about the formula. Most normal people would have said, "Here Sis, this is how it's done. This is the secret. Why don't you get started too. Make some money. Have a good life." It's not as if it would have cost him anything; it's not as if he would have lost any business that way – he was turning customers away all the time. Am I right or not?'

The interpreter nodded in agreement.

'Of course I'm right – just look what happened. What good did it all do him? Swallowed up by a lion along with his precious formula.'

'Swallowed up by a lion? Whatever do you mean?'

'Some people round here think he was eaten by a lion.'

'Are there lions on this island?'

'Most definitely.'

T. Rosenmann squeezed the interpreter's wrist.

'I demand to know what is being said.'

'She says that people say that he was eaten by lions.'

'What lions?'

'Indigenous lions.'

'Indigenous to this island?'

'Of course,' said the interpreter casually.

'Are you pulling my leg?'

'No, I am simply providing a translation.'

'What's he saying?' asked E. Rodakis.

'The lion factor, Madam, made an impression on the gentleman.'

'Is she out of her mind?'

'Possibly.'

'His daughter,' exclaimed T. Rosenmann suddenly, annoyed at himself for not having thought about her sooner. 'Ask her where the daughter is.'

'The gentleman would like to know where your brother's daughter, your niece, can be found.'

'She disappeared too.'

'She disappeared too.'

'It's obvious – they must have left the island together,' concluded T. Rosenmann.

'No. They didn't go missing at the same time,' said E. Rodakis, as though she understood what had been said. 'First my brother vanished and then the girl. She didn't really disappear; she just left. That's why I found the house closed up and all her things gone. I was going to ask the priest; he knows everyone's business, but he's dead too. I have no idea where she went. Maybe to some relative on her mother's side; I really don't know.'

The interpreter interpreted. As he listened, T. Rosenmann's eyes were drawn to a small round box with a lion's head carved on the lid.

'I remember that box. Tell her that her brother showed it to me when I stayed here.'

When she heard that T. Rosenmann had been to the house before, she was puzzled.

'The gentleman knows your brother. And your niece. He was their guest two years ago.'

'I've decided to move up here in the summers, otherwise the house will fall apart. It needs a lot of work. And it's too out of the way for my husband to get to work from here. That box, yes, I found it stuffed away inside one of the cupboards along with a lot of other things. I emptied it, put all the things on display around the house to cheer the place up a bit. It's very cool here in the summer.'

On T. Rosenmann's instructions, the interpreter asked her if she had any other information about her brother that might be relevant.

'Like I told you. Nobody knows anything. It was as if the earth opened up and swallowed him whole. I did everything I could: fasted for three weeks; took communion and left an offering at the Site. But nothing.'

'What did she say?'

'Nobody knows anything. She fasted, took communion, and did something else that I didn't understand,' he said and then, turning to the woman:

'What offering did you leave?'

'I left an offering at the Site – it's the monastery with the hollow hill. So he'd be found.'

'She went to a monastery and prayed,' he explained, giving T. Rosenmann the short version.

T. Rosenmann motioned to the interpreter to leave. It was clear that the sister had nothing further to tell them. They thanked her and left, while she scratched her chin, upset that they did not want to stay and chat.

Bumping along in the cart, doing his best to quell his nausea, the interpreter couldn't help but think how this trip was not living up to his expectations. When an old acquaintance of his had got in touch, telling him that a certain Mr Rosenmann was looking for an interpreter fluent in the language and who would be willing to accompany him to the island on business for two days, three at the most, he jumped at the chance. No matter that he wasn't a professional interpreter; a trip in the height of summer, all expenses paid in addition to his fee, might turn out to be the refreshing getaway he needed to escape from his humdrum existence. But during the journey, as T. Rosenmann briefed him on the nature of the transaction, filling him in on Angelico and the eccentric Rodakis, he had a sense of foreboding about the whole thing. He would have been much more comfortable with the sale of a piece of land or an import-export agreement, of the kind that takes place everyday everywhere in the civilised world. He did not like things to be out of the ordinary.

His disenchantment didn't stop there: He and T. Rosenmann arrive at the island in the middle of the day but instead of getting down to business, they waste a great deal of time, putting everything off until the following day, when he's woken up at the crack of dawn, and is barely given enough time to shave. Then he's forced to walk for hours, which he hates doing, and makes an enormous effort to mask his displeasure and to be good company. At last they reach their destination, only to discover that the prospective partner in their negotiations has been missing for a year: no contact or arrangements have been made in advance. Instead, they meet a slightly unstable woman, the man's sister, who is of no help whatsoever. They are ready to leave after this fruitless visit, when T. Rosenmann suddenly changes his mind. It comes to him in a flash, or so he says, from something Rodakis's sister said, that she went to pray at a monastery (if he had the slightest inkling of the effect these words were to have, there is no way he would have translated them). He is now determined to visit one of the island's monasteries to try to find some antique or other, even if he has to bribe some vulnerable monk to get one, either to keep or to give as a gift to his friend the baron. They make enquiries and are told that there are three monasteries on the island, and of course Mr Rosenmann has to choose the one that is furthest away, on account of its fascinating history, so he says. He realises as soon as he hears its name, the Site, that it must be the same monastery that E. Rodakis had mentioned. Thus, after another night at the pension, they find themselves in yet another vehicle of dubious roadworthiness, jolting along since dawn along the bumpy lanes; only this time he is not about to play the part of the cheery travel companion: he is sitting on a dusty old sack of bran, in silence, nervously digging a fingernail into the rind of a lemon he found rolling along the floor of the cart.

T. Rosenmann could not be expected to read the thoughts of his interpreter. However, observing him out of the corner of his eye, he could see that he was not in the best of moods. It occurred to him that something might be bothering him. Not at all impossible – after all he had spend the best part of his life for the last few decades shut up inside the four walls of a sunless study, so it would be understandable if all this sunlight had got to him and he was longing to go home, like a mole, seeking out the comfort of his underground warrens. His nose, red from the sun, his ginger goatee together with his disgruntled expression, all contributed to a rather comical picture. T. Rosenmann was sorely tempted to have a bit of fun with the man – tweak his cheek, or stick a twig in his ear. Fortunately, he did not give in to these impulses. Besides, he wasn't in the best of moods himself; he had arrived on the island with such a sense of anticipation, and his failure to find Rodakis had depressed him immensely. He was hoping to leave the island with some kind of charming acquisition in his luggage, at the very least.

The guide who had agreed to take them up to the Site in his cart deposited his passengers as soon as the hill came into view, explaining that the path would soon be too narrow for his cart. He reassured them that the walk would be ten minutes at most. T. Rosenmann paid the man the agreed sum; he stuffed the money deep inside his trouser pocket and installed himself under a big tree, produced a tomato on a napkin and started eating. He confirmed that he would wait as long as necessary and would take them back, as agreed.

The two men had not gone far when a noise was heard. They turned round only to see the man hurrying off with his cart. The interpreter called after him but soon realised how pointless it was.

'We shouldn't have paid him.'

'He might come back.'

'No he won't. Didn't you see him pretend to wait under a tree and try to convince us that he'd wait all day – and then the minute we turned our backs...?'

'Anyway, we shouldn't let this unpleasant event spoil our mood. We'll find some other way to get back.'

And with a spring in his step, which the interpreter thought totally unsuited to the occasion, T. Rosenmann started walking up towards the monastery on a path that showed absolutely no signs of narrowing at any point; if anything it became wider and more regular the closer they came to the Site. They were at the monastery within ten minutes. On that point at least, the guide had been truthful.

A monk, who had spotted them from a long way off approached, obviously intrigued (if not downright suspicious) by the sight of these two extraordinary characters, and asked them what they wanted. The interpreter translated for T. Rosenmann, who took a step closer to the monk, touched his shoulder, and with a passion quite out of keeping with his temperament and unsuited to the occasion, spoke to him in a language that was completely incomprehensible to the young monk. Taken aback, he turned to the interpreter, who, right on cue, began to translate

T. Rosenmann's effusive monologue.

'It gives me such joy to find myself on this hallowed ground! For years I have been trying to make this journey, but always encountered obstacles at the last moment. But now I am here, at last, walking on this sacred corner of the earth. Glorious is Thy name, O Lord!'

He knelt down, and kissed the first stone that came into his line of vision. The interpreter meanwhile, swept away on this tide of religious fervour, managed to make the sign of the cross without neglecting his linguistic duties for one moment.

'I have heard so much about your divinely-inspired work up here, a labour of love that you monks have devoted yourselves to for centuries, chiselling away inside the hollow hillside, a miracle of human achievement, dedicated to the glorification of God in the highest. My desire to see this monumental work with my own eyes consumes me. How I long to leave this island taking with me just one tiny little stone from your excavations. Give me leave to admire your creation, I implore you.'

The monk was unmoved. He told them that he did not have the authority to permit such visits; the abbot was feeling indisposed and should not be disturbed on any account. He made it clear that visitors were forbidden to enter the Site, and with the exception of the monks, only one person had ever been allowed to cross its threshold. T. Rosenmann appeared to take this news to heart, but said that he was hopeful nevertheless, and since an exception had been made in the past, there was no reason why another should not be made in the future. The monk merely shrugged his shoulders.

The interpreter, on his own initiative, asked the monk to communicate his companion's request to whoever was responsible for such matters, and explain why it was of such great importance to him. With evident cunning and a conspiratorial expression, he told the monk that the gentleman who had just arrived from overseas was very wealthy and generous to those who showed him their support. T. Rosenmann, understanding perfectly well what the interpreter was doing, feigned innocence and asked for a translation. The interpreter smiled reassuringly, and shot a most conniving look at the young monk who responded with an impassive stare. They were told to sit and wait under the shade of a pine tree while the monk turned and walked off in the direction of the monastery.

Before long, Anthimos appeared and greeted them warmly. He said that the young monk had informed them of their arrival and had communicated their wish to visit the Site. This, unfortunately, was quite out of the question, and he refused to yield to the interpreter's desperate pleas. He said that since they had come all that way, they could visit the chapel and the monastery, although they were not of any particular architectural interest. The interpreter, anxious to bring this exhausting mission to a close, employed the same tactic he had used with the young monk, only more pointed this time, leaving no doubt that the well-to-do gentleman standing next to him would be immensely grateful to anyone who could secure an attractive souvenir of the monastery – an icon or a vessel, perhaps a manuscript, since his hopes of visiting the hill had been dashed. The look of astounded fury that crossed Anthimos's face ruled out any such transaction, and the interpreter was forced to change tack.

The two men followed the monk into the church. While the interpreter listened to Anthimos talk about the murals in the cupola, T. Rosenmann plucked a silver offering depicting a baby in swaddling clothes from one of the icons, and quickly secreted it in his pocket.

'Do you happen to know anything at all about the disappearance of a local man, a Mr Rodakis?' asked the interpreter as the three of them were leaving the church.

This bolt from the blue sent Anthimos into a state of blind panic.

'Why do you ask?'

'Mr Rodakis is an old acquaintance of the gentleman's. When

we called on him, his sister told us that he had disappeared – unbelievable. She suspects that the lions which reportedly move freely on the island are to blame.'

'News of his disappearance reached us too. Nobody knows any more than that.'

Something in his voice betrayed his unease, but the interpreter did not pick up on it. The monk had passed over the issue of the lions without comment, so the interpreter brought it up again.

'Do you monks believe that lions roam the island?'

'Some do. I don't.'

He told them to sit down again on the stone bench under the pine tree and enjoy the breeze while he went to get them something to eat.

The bright summer day did not penetrate the silence or the darkness of the abbot's bedroom. He could no longer tolerate intense light or loud noise, so despite their agitation and inability to agree on a course of action, the three monks huddled over his bed spoke in hushed voices. Their movements were exaggerated, their body language emphatic; their spasmodic gestures hovered above the recumbent abbot like vultures circling a carcass, waiting for the right moment to descend.

The arrival of the two strangers was responsible for this commotion. The monks all doubted that the foreigners knew what was going on. But on the other hand, nobody could be completely sure that Rodakis's old acquaintances had not started an investigation into his disappearance which had led them to the monastery. They should not forget that Rodakis was in possession of a uniquely profitable concept, and a great many people might be willing to move heaven and earth to find him. This fact alone automatically cast suspicion on the two foreigners.

While they were agreed on all these points, they could not agree on how best to deal with the situation. Anthimos said that as soon as the visitors finished eating they should be asked to leave because the Site was not a tourist attraction.

The second monk to speak – Paschalis – argued that that would be the worst thing they could do, as it would only make the men even more suspicious. He suggested inviting them to stay as long as they wished and giving them the impression that they were indifferent to their presence. Naturally, they would be watched like hawks, until their intentions were clear. The third monk, the monk with the bulging forehead, adopted the most extreme position, dismissing the previous suggestions as non-solutions. He insisted on apprehending and imprisoning the two men, and releasing them only if they could prove under interrogation that their arrival had nothing to do with the Rodakis case.

The abbot, who had been following the discussion carefully, spoke next. First of all he instructed Anthimos and Paschalis (the only monks who held the keys to the Error Room) to put a stop to Rodakis's daily walk. He further required Anthimos (who alone had the key to the main entrance to the Site), to be even more vigilant than usual, and if he felt it necessary, halt the work to the dome. Then he turned to the arguments mooted by the three monks, and without hesitation gave his support to Paschalis's proposal of discreet surveillance. As an afterthought, he added an idea of his own, and left its implementation to Paschalis, in his view the most capable of the monks. His mission would be to befriend the two strangers, by pretending to be a half-wit living on the monastery's charity: somebody like that, so easy to manipulate, would guarantee direct access to inside information, an opportunity the two men (if they were indeed looking for information) would not fail to exploit.

Paschalis did not need detailed instructions; he immediately understood the purpose of his task. As soon as the brief council adjourned, he dashed to the forecourt of the monastery and approached the stone bench just as the two men were finishing up their meal. He lurked behind a tree, ostensibly keeping out of sight, and watched them, all the while shuffling so noisily that it was impossible for him to escape their notice.

The interpreter gave T. Rosenmann a nudge. Moving his eyebrows in the direction of the tree, T. Rosenmann spotted a head pop out and disappear again behind the trunk of the tree, its expression ranging from serious to inane.

'Hello there!' shouted the interpreter after spitting an olive stone onto the ground.

A figure emerged very slowly and very timidly from behind the tree, its mouth now set in the inane grin. Swaying slightly, the strange creature pointed and said:

'Me olives.'

The interpreter, thinking the man wanted an olive, handed him the platter, and invited him to take one, a gesture which was met with a decisive shake of the head.

'Me pick olives.'

'I see! You picked these,' and then in a whisper to T. Rosenmann, 'The man's a simpleton.'

'Me pick olives off olive trees,' repeated the creature and promptly collapsed into fits of hysterical giggles.

This was how T. Rosenmann and his interpreter became acquainted with Paschalis. They sat together for some time until it got too hot. There was no real conversation; most of the time the two strangers whispered and muttered to each other in their own language. Occasionally the interpreter would turn to him and say a few words, either teasingly, or in the tone people adopt when addressing very small children. Paschalis took this as confirmation that he was putting on a convincing show. Nonetheless, they never once tried to get any information out of him; Rodakis's name never once crossed their lips.

When the heat became intolerable, Paschalis showed them to the monastery balcony and the conversation took an unexpected turn.

'Aren't you afraid of lions?'

He shook his head.

'Scared of snakes. And wasps. And scorpions. Not scared of lions.'

'Didn't you hear about that man – from this island – Rodakis? He was eaten alive, right down to the last bone in his body, by lions. They drank every last drop of his blood too. That's why they never found his body.'

In an effort to make the whole scene even more macabre and scare the wits out of the idiot, he added:

'The only thing they didn't touch was his hair, but it was scattered to the winds.'

'Not true. It's not. No lions. Aren't any lions. That's just stories, that's what I say.'

'You've got more sense than most of them. What nonsense – eaten by lions! It doesn't take a genius to realise that the man ran away.'

'Why you want Rodakis?' asked Paschalis, all innocence.

'I don't. He does,' said the interpreter, pointing to T. Rosenmann, who had not the slightest interest in engaging the backward monk in conversation, and was admiring the sea view instead. The interpreter continued, stressing his words:

'He's an extremely wealthy man. Extremely. He wants to do business with Mr Rodakis. Have you ever seen such a rich person in all your life? Have you?'

'What rich man want?' he said, daring to ask the crucial question.

'Look – if you can bring us a beautiful old piece of whatever you keep hidden away in the monastery, so we can take home a nice souvenir home with us, the gentleman will give you your very own piece of gold, big as a chestnut.'

Paschalis rolled his eyes in feigned excitement.

'Mine – for keeps?'

'I've seen it; it's in his pocket. If he likes what you bring him, it's yours.'

'Tonight.'

'We'll have left by then.'

'Tonight. Sleep here. I come tonight.'

With that, he vanished. Paschalis concluded that although the two foreigners clearly had an interest in Rodakis, they had not come all the way up to the Site looking for him. They were after something else.

The interpreter repeated the conversation to T. Rosenmann, who was pleased with the turn things had taken, and congratulated him on the way he had handled the simpleton monk. Nobody else approached them until late in the evening when a young novice appeared and asked if they needed somewhere to sleep. They accepted happily and were shown to the guestroom.

The interpreter instantly fell into a deep sleep, but T. Rosenmann on hearing the door close, suddenly became extremely uneasy and agitated. This was not due to his impatience to see what the slow-witted monk would bring him; it was more a concern that the idiot would botch the job and wake the entire monastery. The possibility had not occurred to him before, and was starting to worry him. He looked at his interpreter, lying there fast asleep, his mouth wide open, oblivious to all this. The mere sight of him made T. Rosenmann's blood boil. He recalled their journey up to the Site in the cart during which they had been in the opposite situation: he had been calm while the interpreter had been stewing in his own juices. He wondered whether this was the other man's way of paying him back.

This went on for hours, with no change either in his mood or in the imperturbable calm of the Site at night.

Just before midnight, a rhythmic banging noise was heard, rather like a pre-arranged signal. The interpreter didn't stir even when his employer gave him a vigorous shove as he moved towards the door. Seeing Paschalis alone, T. Rosenmann heaved a sigh of relief.

Paschalis hurried inside the cell, anxious not to be seen.

Without even looking at T. Rosenmann, he strode across to the sleeping figure of the interpreter. After a few ineffectual pushes and prods, he administered a violent slap to his face, which had the interpreter awake in a flash. Stunned, he looked up to see Paschalis bending over him, in a state of agitation, telling him to wake up. Putting this down to his mental incapacity, the victim decided to overlook this barbaric behaviour and get down to business.

'What have you got for us?'

'Tell your friend I've got something he'll like a lot,' he snapped.

The interpreter turned and looked at T. Rosenmann, who, standing in the opposite corner of the cell, was equally dumbfounded. Although he had not understood a word of the exchange, he had realised from the first moment he saw him that there was something different about the monk, as though he was a completely different person, no matter that he looked just like the man they'd been talking to a few hours earlier. His voice was steady and commanding, his eyes lucid. The rocking motion of his body had gone and his movements were perfectly coordinated.

The interpreter translated flatly.

'He's got something I'd like a lot?' repeated T. Rosenmann. 'And what might that be?'

The interpreter put the question to Paschalis who crossed the cell and went to stand next to T. Rosenmann.

'Rodakis,' he said, pronouncing the name as clearly as he could.

The idea of handing Rodakis over to the rich foreigner had come to Paschalis only a few hours before he went down to the guestroom. Before that, he had been trying to think of a way to teach him a lesson, to pay him back for having the gall to suggest that he could walk out with a holy monastery relic, washed in the blood of generations past, in exchange for money. After he had calmed down a little, he decided that teaching the man a lesson was less urgent than other opportunities the circumstances could yield – opportunities relating to the monastery prisoner.

When he reviewed the situation, he had to confess that Rodakis's incarceration had not proceeded satisfactorily. Stubborn as anything, he had kept his lips sealed, and the way things were going, would more likely die than give away his secret. As time went on, he seemed less and less likely to crack, and was suffering from depression. He had no appetite for anything and gave the impression of having abandoned all interest in life, and to be waiting on some kind of *deus ex machina* solution to his problem: anything but capitulate. This sort of resignation led to the shrivelling of the soul, and the shrivelling of the soul led to death.

This development did not please Paschalis. He might have been the architect of Rodakis's predicament, but revenge had not been his only motive (he'd always been honest about that and had admitted as much to Rodakis during their chance encounter); all he wanted was the formula, as he felt that he had contributed to it in some way. He wanted it out of the hands of one individual to serve the common good. But that would never happen if Rodakis ended up mad or dead. The unexpected arrival of the two rich foreigners on the island, looking for the famous bee-keeper to go into partnership with, and their chance visit to the monastery lit the way for a new solution to the problem.

If Rodakis agreed – even if it meant holding on to his secret – to go into business with the rich foreigner, and if he, as the go-between, produced the man the rich foreigner was looking for and offered Rodakis his freedom, then he would be entitled to a handsome commission. With it, he would be able to do something of social value, even, in this indirect way, to fulfil his original aim. He would be able to provide relief to widows and orphans, restore old churches, build bridges or – and this idea excited him more than anything – leave the Site and establish his own monastery.

He'd start with the foreigner and ensure that he got a satisfactory cut. If there was one thing he'd learnt all this time in the monastery, it was how to conduct successful business deals. Wrong. There was something else too: never ignore the signs, never be indifferent or blind or deaf to them. T. Rosenmann's arrival was an opportunity crying out to be seized.

If his discussion with the foreigner had the desired outcome, his next move would be to extract a commitment from Rodakis to cooperate. He really had very little choice. Then he would have to arrange his escape from the Site – and that was not going to be easy. He had the key to the Error Room; only Anthimos and the abbot had the keys to the main gates.

Paschalis saw that the path he had mapped out was not only long and difficult but also fraught with risk. Nevertheless, he decided to pursue it, and like any wise general, established a plan of action.

The opening of the hole in the middle of the dome was scheduled to be cut the following week. It would be a significant moment in the long history of the monastery, marking the end of an era started by the first dent left by the old anchorite's chisel on the wall of the small cave. Over the successive centuries, one of the most powerful and most historic monasteries in the country had grown up, its name and progress becoming tied over time with the divinely inspired construction of a complex edifice in the hill's interior. This achievement, despite the perpetuation of its reputation, remained invisible to the eyes of the world, beyond the vast wrought-iron door at the foot of an otherwise very ordinary hill, with its low-lying vegetation, its butterflies, lizards, hedgehogs roaming around on the outside.

The imminent completion of the Site did not, however, create a holiday mood in the hearts of those working on it. On the contrary, as the end drew near, the Site was enshrouded in an atmosphere of mourning. The monks moved about with long faces, gloomy and sullen, while everyone working inside deliberately dragged their feet, as though trying to forestall the inevitable. The excavation of the hill, an inseparable part of life at the monastery, was coming to an end, leaving the monks with the sense that a part of them had been amputated. Several of them had expressed the wish to embark on a new, equally ambitious project – the construction of a network of underground tunnels or building a church entirely out of tiny pebbles.

It would take approximately six days to perfect the opening in the ceiling, which was almost exactly the central point of the hill. During this time, the hole would remain open, waiting for the blacksmith to come and install some iron bars and a heavy metal covering over it, which could be lifted and closed like a lid. The bars were for security reasons; the lid was designed to protect the Site in case of flooding.

This hole was a temporary Achilles heel in the heart of the Site, and was taken as yet another sign by Paschalis, particularly in view of the timing. This was his only hope of getting Rodakis out of the Site, and it was as if fate had extended a helping hand.

So, once T. Rosenmann agreed to Paschalis's terms, and when Rodakis, deep within the pale fog that enveloped him, alienated from everything and everybody, gave his answer – which, in all its vagueness appeared to be positive – the planning went into the final stage, that of plotting the escape. Paschalis, as someone who worked on the dome every day, as well as the abbot's most trusted monk, was well placed to determine the best time for it to take place.

T. Rosenmann, who had left the island to avoid arousing suspicion, returned on the appointed day, and, around midnight, set off for the hilltop, dressed in dark clothing. The interpreter, accompanying him on this occasion too, stayed behind, waiting for them at a small bay used by the monastery. Paschalis appeared a short while after T. Rosenmann, holding a thick rope. The two men nodded a silent greeting. T. Rosenmann waited for Paschalis to give him the signal to start the necessary procedure, but instead, Paschalis remained silent and still as though he had been struck by lightning. This was worrying; he approached, but Paschalis raised his hand to deter him from coming any closer. He stood there, frozen. When he made the sign of the cross all of a sudden, T. Rosenmann realised that Paschalis had been praying all along.

Then he knelt down and bent over the hole, after first removing the makeshift covering of wooden planks. Sticking his head into the opening he made a sound somewhere between a whistle and a squawk. It was not returned. He whistle-squawked again. Again there was no reply.

'What the hell is going on?' he murmured, clearly unsettled. He thought for a while and then said:

'I'd better go down there myself.'

He carefully wound the rope round a slab of rock jutting out of the ground, with such a practised hand that it was obvious that he had rehearsed it frequently. With impressive speed, he lowered himself into the dark cavity. As soon as his feet made contact with a hard surface, he lit the small candle he always kept hanging from the cord of his cassock. Rodakis was supposed to be waiting for him. Paschalis had given him clear instructions only a few hours before when he took him his evening meal. On his way out he went through the motions of turning the key, and left the cell unlocked. But there was nobody there. Paschalis hurried along to the Error Room, and looking behind its half-open door, found it empty. He didn't know what to think. Quite at random, he chose the passageway leading to the library and there, approximately half way along, spotted Rodakis squatting down with his back against the wall, asleep. He shook him until he woke with a start, asking if it was time.

Paschalis wondered how it was possible that someone could sleep at a time like this; another instance of Rodakis's recent bizarre behaviour.

They went up to the dome. Paschalis held onto the rope and, squashing his body up like a caterpillar, climbed up to the opening. He motioned to Rodakis that the coast was clear and that it was his turn to ascend. He grabbed the rope with his hands and his teeth while the men outside hoisted him slowly to the surface.

He was free. For the first time in ages he was able to see the sky above and the sea below. The darkness didn't make any difference; he could hear it very clearly. T. Rosenmann squeezed his hand warmly, and he cried out in pain. Paschalis, who was anxious not to waste time, motioned to them not to speak but to follow him.

They went down the hillside and took a footpath, which was quite regular and easy to follow despite the darkness until they reached the spot where the interpreter was waiting for them. Paschalis led them to a boat half hidden among the rocks, and took the helm. They set off for the main harbour where they were due to transfer to a large merchant ship which was scheduled to set sail for the capital a few hours later.

As soon as he heard the plan, Rodakis stood up inside the boat and announced that he refused to go anywhere unless they stopped to pick up Rosa first. Paschalis was forced to tell him that his daughter had left the island a long time ago, and according to the priest's children, she was living with a relative somewhere. Rodakis did not relent: he would not cooperate until he saw his daughter, wherever she was. T. Rosenmann thought this was understandable (but then again, he probably would have found any demand Rodakis cared to make at that moment reasonable), and asked Paschalis if he could tell them anything more about Rosa's whereabouts.

Everything went according to plan: at dawn they embarked on the merchant ship sailing for the capital. They rested and immediately set off to find Rodakis's daughter.

post scriptum

The interpreter was shown to the magistrate's office on the first floor. It was empty. He sat down on a tattered old leather armchair opposite an oak desk creaking under the weight of all the papers piled up on it; behind that was the examining magistrate's chair, made of the same worn out leather. Everything in the room, from the furniture to the random placement of various objects after their last use, gave the visitor a clear sense of its occupant. When the examining magistrate walked in a few minutes later and sat down at his desk, his shiny pate, his spectacles, his greasy skin and his chubby fingers blended in perfectly against this backdrop. His chair looked like it had been cast from a mould taken from his back with the precision of a tailor during a final fitting of a jacket.

His fingers automatically found out the relevant papers in the pile. He was not intending to spend much time on this witness; his cat had been taken ill, and his only concern was to get back to it as quickly as possible. In a bid to pre-empt any preamble and unnecessary chatter, he began his interrogation with precisely formulated questions, all requiring brief, precisely formulated answers. Unfortunately, this witness was not the most laconic he'd ever interviewed, and would preface all his answers thus: 'I can't answer that before I have explained…' or thus, 'My answer will be meaningless if I do not first refer you to…' or thus: 'If you'll allow me to take things from the beginning…'

This was beginning to irritate the examining magistrate. Getting information out of most witnesses was like getting blood out of stone. But this one, not only was he the most garrulous witness he had ever questioned, but seemed bent on going through everything in exhausting detail. In addition to his blow-by-blow account of events, he insisted on providing minute character portraits of every individual involved in the case. Nevertheless, the examining magistrate's impatience to draw the interview to a speedy conclusion began to weaken as the minutes ticked by. He wasn't sure whether this was the result of the very vivid way in which the witness made his statement, or if it was the extraordinary facts of the case itself that were drawing him into the story to the point where he was totally fascinated by everything connected to the case, however remotely.

'The fact is,' said the interpreter in a rare hiatus in his narrative, 'I never got to try the famous honey, and am therefore unable to comment on its merits or judge whether all the fuss was justified. What I do know is that that man, Rodakis, was looked on by everyone as the goose that laid the golden eggs. Everybody wanted to control him. When we finally discovered his whereabouts in the monastery, that unbelievable coincidence I told you about, my employer – Mr Rosenmann – told me very clearly that under no circumstances must I tell anyone I knew where he was, so that everybody would go on believing that he had disappeared. His concern was completely unfounded, as I had no contact whatsoever with the locals. On our second visit to the island, when we were planning to rescue him and to smuggle him out with the monk's help, Rosenmann was very concerned about maintaining the utmost secrecy. For that reason he made me wear a female disguise and travel with him as his wife so that nobody at the harbour would be able to recognise us from our previous visit. He made do with a simple beard, while I spent the entire journey wondering why I had been so foolish as to agree to such an absurd caper in the first place. At least the rescue mission was a success; and I was spared any further humiliation.

We boarded a very rickety vessel. Had the sea not been completely still that night, I'm sure we would have sunk without trace within the first nautical mile. We reached the harbour and transferred to a merchant ship. The monk changed out of his cassock and snipped off his beard. Rodakis donned the discarded cassock and played the role of the monk. All of this took place on that dubious vessel. When we got to the port, we split off into pairs, the monk and Rodakis, and the married couple. Needless to say (but I'll say it anyway) every time Rodakis looked at me, he would burst into fits of uncontrollable laughter – shame I didn't have a mirror to show him what a pitiful condition he was in himself. After the boat left the harbour, I changed my clothes at the first possible opportunity, but even then, the man was beside himself with merriment as soon as he saw me, so out of control that he could hardly breathe, and we were all concerned that something was seriously wrong with him.'

'How did you all come to be guests at the baron's estate?' asked the magistrate in an attempt to redirect the witness.

'That was much later on,' explained the interpreter. 'Rodakis made his cooperation conditional on seeing his daughter, who was living in a city somewhere on the mainland. My employer didn't want to risk losing Rodakis, and decided that we should go with him. The monk came too. He had interests to protect. Nobody trusted anybody; everybody was suspicious of everybody else. Working on the information the monk had, we managed to track down the man's daughter. She was part of a very peculiar set up. She was living with some ancient, bedridden relative of hers, and an old woman (the housekeeper, judging by what the monk said). The extraordinary thing was that these two old crocks – and I never found out why – kept her locked up in her room all the time, something that didn't seem to bother her unduly. Rosenmann and I didn't go up into the house, so I don't know what the old man and Rodakis said to each other. But I don't rule out the possibility that the girl was taken by force; Rodakis and the monk both emerged from the house looking very flushed. The girl was totally disorientated, initially at least. She gradually regained her spirit and was clearly very pleased to see Mr Rodakis again.'

'After the bee-keeper's demand to find his daughter had been met, did he begin some preliminary negotiations with Mr Rosenmann?'

'Not immediately. Not that day. Rodakis hadn't seen his daughter for so long, and she had written him off, so you can imagine her astonishment and her joy. All we did that day was find somewhere to spend the night nearby. Rosenmann footed the bill for everybody, and we didn't discuss anything with Rodakis that evening: he and his daughter were inseparable anyway. The following morning all the men met in the dining room.

Rosenmann came straight to the point, asking Rodakis when and where they would start, but before the man had a chance to answer, the monk leapt to his feet, demanding to determine his share of the future income before anything else was agreed on. He was most impertinent, I don't mind saying. I could see Mr Rosenmann's blood boiling, but he managed to remain calm and controlled, and informed the monk that the agreement they had made at the monastery stood. The monk then pushed for an advance payment; Rosenmann looked daggers at him and told him he had never made any such undertaking and if the monk didn't like it, nobody would weep if he withdrew from the partnership. That put him in his place and he didn't dare open his mouth for a long time after that.

After Rosenmann dealt with the monk, we turned to Rodakis and saw that he was white as a ghost. I suspected that something was amiss; unfortunately I was right. He looked at Rosenmann and said, "However much I would like to do business with you, it is quite out of the question — at least for the time being. I am unable to recall the formula." You could have heard a pin drop. Rodakis had forgotten the secret formula! But this was the first time he'd mentioned it. We had gone to all that trouble for nothing.'

'Although I cannot see how all this is remotely connected to the case,' said the examining magistrate, 'did it not occur to any of you that this might just have been a trick to keep the secret formula to himself?'

'Naturally that was the first thought to cross our minds. But if you had seen the look of despair on his face, you would not have doubted his sincerity.'

'It's hard to believe that someone would invest so much time and effort into developing something as important as that without keeping clear records of the method employed.'

'Arrogance is a serious defect of character, and Rodakis had more than his fair share of it. He was confident that he would never forget the formula in the same way that one never forgets one's name. He explained that he had codified the names and quantities of the plants in the form of a short rhyme, from which it was possible to derive the formula. He never imagined that it would be possible for him to forget the rhyme. But he did.'

'Please stick to the facts.'

'This is all necessary background information; you need to understand why we decided to take Rodakis and his daughter back with us.'

'You didn't just take them back, you installed them on the baron's estate.'

'Precisely.'

The interpreter continued:

'As I told you before, we were sceptical at first about this sudden memory loss, but then we reasoned that had he wanted to pull out of the arrangement, he could have done so without feigning amnesia. There was nothing in writing after all, and if he had decided to leave with his daughter, nobody would have detained him by force. We were hopeful, however, that it would come back to him. Mr Rosenmann in particular believed it was only a matter of time. His optimism stemmed from the fact that only a few days before Rodakis announced that he had forgotten the rhyme, he had remembered the formula and had been over it in his mind. Rosenmann tried to work out what could have happened in the intervening time to cause him to forget. He could not pinpoint anything. It had to be psychological in origin; at some point his mind stopped working. It happens all the time. We often find ourselves unable to remember the name of our closest friends, or a place we've visited umpteen times, but we don't think anything of it, because we know that it will come back to us sooner or later. But Rodakis was panicking, so much so that from that point onwards, he couldn't remember a thing. He would wake up and go to sleep worrying about it and however hard he racked his brains, he could only manage to drag a few unconnected words and phrases to the surface.

The monk just sat there, shaking his head as he listened, which was extremely irritating. When Mr Rosenmann asked why he kept doing it and he replied that this explained Rodakis's recent condition; how he had seemed unwell. This made us even more convinced that Rodakis was telling the truth. But Rosenmann is not one to admit defeat. He informed Rodakis that the problem was psychological and as soon as he calmed down, it would all come back to him.

To facilitate this, he suggested to Rodakis that he and his daughter spend some time as guests of his old friend the baron. Rosenmann was sure that the luxurious, beautiful surroundings would help soothe Rodakis's troubled mind. Of course he was right. If you take into account the appalling conditions Rodakis had been living in, caged up in that cave, the baron's estate would look like paradise in comparison. Rodakis accepted the invitation, largely thanks to his daughter; she was very excited by the idea of a long journey, and started jumping up and down, begging him to say yes. Rosenmann had been careful to tell her all about the colourful rooms and the lake with the wild geese before putting the idea to her father. That's how, before we really knew what was going on, we all ended up together on the estate.

I should add that Mr Rosenmann had contracted my services as his interpreter for the duration of one year, at a rate two and half times higher than my previous employer. You can see from that how determined the man was. I would have been a fool to turn him down. Mr Rosenmann is still paying me, even now, although he is not using me at all. A true gentleman.'

'The facts.'

'The baron received us warmly. I couldn't tell whether he was hospitable by nature or whether he was simply fascinated by this affair of the honey. I assume that you will need to draw up the profile of each person involved in this case, and to enable you to do so, I'll tell you about what took place that first evening at the estate. Rodakis, up to that point, I'd liked. He seemed like a good, decent sort. But to my astonishment, that evening, it became clear that the man was an utter bastard; totally corrupt and degenerate. How else can one describe a man who indulges in sexual intercourse with his own flesh and blood, with his own daughter? I'd be prepared to file an official report. I am a witness; I saw them with my own eyes, in the yellow room – the one the girl was staying in. I was in the dark green one and Rodakis in the blue. Rosenmann had the most attractive room, a gentle shade of purple. I went to him immediately and told him everything. I was understandably distraught. After listening calmly, he told me that the incident was none of our concern. I won't pretend that this made me suspect that the only thing that concerned Mr Rosenmann was this business with the honey and that he would turn a blind eye even if the most heinous crime were to take place under his very nose. During those ten days at the baron's estate, I was aware of two further incidents. I chide myself constantly for not obeying my conscience and teaching the bastard a lesson he'll never forget. But I was worried that I'd upset the deal and have to take the blame for Rodakis's amnesia and everything else that had gone wrong.'

'Let's leave this not insignificant fact to one side for the moment,' said the examining magistrate. 'I must ask you to kindly restrict yourself to the ten days spent on the baron's estate, and to try to recall if anything unusual or suspect came to your attention during that time.'

'Suspect no. Nothing, that is, that I could connect with the case. No, I cannot say that I was aware of anything like that; it would be untruthful of me to say that I was. As for unusual… everything about the Rodakis duo was unusual. One evening while I was in my room preparing to retire, there was a gentle knock on my door. It was the young girl. She was holding the key to her room and begged me to take her back to her room and lock her in. At first I was unable to understand what she meant; I thought she needed help with her lock, but in fact she wanted me to lock her in because she wouldn't be able to get to sleep otherwise – or so she said. Her father usually locked her in, but she didn't want to disturb him. When I asked her why she needed to sleep with a locked door, she told me that she was locked up at night in her last house and had grown to like it. Apparently it made her feel safe. I told her that I could understand that but what I couldn't understand was why she didn't just lock herself in. Do you know what she said? She said, "If someone else has got the key, that makes them responsible for me, and that's what makes me feel secure." What could I say to that? I duly turned the key and handed it to her father first thing in the morning. She'd become accustomed to being a prisoner and when she regained her freedom, she started to miss it. The truth is, after I found out about them, the incest, I mean, I kept my distance from both father and daughter, and kept conversation with them to a minimum. I was happy to offer my services when needed, but this happened only seldom as Mr Rosenmann did not want Rodakis to feel any pressure, so we tried to be as discreet as possible. When

we were all together, a number of subjects were discussed, but never honey, never the island, never his past, never the past, unless the conversation turned to inventors, prophets or seafarers – some of Rodakis's favourite topics.

As for the burning issue of the formula, we steered clear of it. We were just a carefree group of friends on holiday, and nothing was allowed to compromise our calm. Of course I didn't have any reason to object; on the contrary. I was enjoying a holiday in the countryside, and was, moreover, being remunerated for my pains. The person who was most at ease there was Rodakis. He ate well, drank a great deal, and roamed around the estate as though he owned the place, even giving orders to the domestic staff. He was utterly insufferable. His cheeks had filled out, and this erstwhile picture of suffering had changed beyond recognition. Either he would walk through the gardens talking nonsense with his daughter, or he'd occupy himself looking through the telescope, or be engrossed in a book about plants (which I think was a gift from those monks). I ought to mention that one day I asked him if I might have a look at his book, and he quickly stuffed it into his pocket and looked at me as though he thought I was going to eat it. He got his comeuppance though; the good Lord saw to that. We can't have been there longer than three days when he was sitting reading it in the dining room, and a servant walked past him carrying a carafe of claret for the baron and Mr Rosenmann. Rodakis suddenly stood up, crashing into the tray as he did so, and bang! Red wine all over his book. He went berserk – tore the whole thing to shreds and threw the sodden fragments up in the air shouting: "Let's be done with this once and for all!" he said. But he salvaged the slipcase. It was beautiful, with the golden outline of an apple tree tooled into the leather.'

'I beg you,' said the examining magistrate in a hoarse voice, 'try to avoid further digressions. They have no bearing on the case. Go on, please.'

'I was describing Rodakis's peculiar behaviour. I couldn't read his mind, but he didn't seem to be concerned about his amnesia any longer. It was as though he had suddenly realised that it was possible to be happy without remembering the formula. That much was obvious, at least to me. I won't pretend that the suspicion that he could recall everything perfectly but was keeping it to himself so that he could continue enjoying himself didn't cross my mind. I can't be sure, and we might never learn the truth. I never dared share these suspicions with Mr Rosenmann, although I did mention to him at some point that I was unimpressed by Rodakis's carefree attitude and felt that he should be trying harder to remember the formula. Rosenmann simply remarked that it was precisely this carefree frame of mind that he was trying to cultivate in Rodakis, because this was the only way he would ever remember. He had convinced the poor baron of this too. I can remember him standing before us repeating Mr Rosenmann's words with great flourish, as though by doing so, he would gain a better understanding of them himself. With sweeping theatrical gestures he announced: "The information we seek is buried deep inside this man's head, as though locked away within four walls. It is not lost. It has not been erased. We simply need to find the way to break down the four walls." So we all waited for the blessed moment when these four walls would come down…'

'Was there any kind of time limit? How long were you all prepared to wait?'

'Nobody set a deadline. I was on contract for one year and it was not my place to opine.'

'During this time, were you aware of any disagreements or arguments between the baron and anybody else – one of the guests or the domestic staff – or anybody else for that matter?'

'No. None at all. From the little I saw of the baron, I could tell that he was not the sort of person who made enemies. Allow me to tell you what I think happened. I do not believe that the baron was murdered. I am quite convinced that his death was accidental.'

'On what grounds?'

'As you know, it was I who discovered the body at dawn on Friday. When I first saw him floating on the surface of the lake, I mistook his body for clothing, a coat perhaps, picked up by the wind and then deposited in the lake. It was not until I was much closer that I realised what it was.'

'What were you doing up and about at that time?' asked the examining magistrate, determined not to allow himself to be sidetracked.

'I had overindulged the previous evening, but it was really the squawking coming from the lake. It was so loud and so persistent that it was quite impossible to sleep, so I decided to give up and get up.'

'You mean to say that…'

'I'm not sure whether the birds had been unsettled on account of the corpse floating in their midst, but they were extremely noisy. Perhaps if it had been a dead duck, they…'

'You have not answered my question. Why are you so sure that the baron's death was accidental?'

'I can't prove it, but I am convinced that one goose in particular was responsible.'

'I beg your pardon?'

'The poor baron (and absolutely anyone on the estate can corroborate this) had recently developed a deep disliking for the goose I refer to. He considered it to be the gaggle troublemaker. I'm serious. He said that it was responsible for all the fighting and disturbances on the lake. I even saw him pelting it with gravel, full of hatred.'

'What are you trying to say? This was "the goose's revenge"?'

'No, no. I think the baron slipped and fell into the water while trying to murder it. It's possible that he'd been woken by the squawking too, and was determined to deal with the troublemaker once and for all. My instinct tells me that it was the goose that brought him down at the lake at that hour. In fact, I'm absolutely certain of it.'

The examining magistrate jotted down the word 'goose' and next to it placed two crosses. After a few more questions, the interrogation was concluded. The interpreter stood up and walked towards the door. He was very proud of himself, considering he had done his duty with a good conscience. He had not tried to incriminate Rodakis, despite his deep loathing for the man. On the contrary, he had presented his own version of events with clarity and honesty. He was more than satisfied with his performance and relished the prospect of being invited back to make a supplementary statement.

As he approached the door, he heard the voice of the examining magistrate behind him:

'One more question before you leave, if you don't mind.'

'Of course.'

'Where do things stand with the bee-keeper? Have all the plans been shelved?'

'I'm sure you will understand that these tragic circumstances have not left us unaffected. My employer in particular was a close friend of the baron's. However, as I told you before, Mr Rosenmann is not one to give up easily, especially when he has set his mind on something. For the time being we are all staying in a hotel waiting for permission to move on to a seaside resort. So you see the plans have not been abandoned.'

'I take it that no progress has been made regarding the bee-keeper's memory?'

'None.'

'Do you personally believe that the situation will change, that he will recall the formula, and if he does recall the formula, he will be willing to cooperate with your employer?'

'Naturally. I may not share Mr Rosenmann's optimism, but I by no means discount the possibility.'

'I have a favour to ask of you,' said the magistrate, noting something on a piece of paper at the same time. 'If and when there is any development, any change at all, please contact me at this address. I must confess, this case has really piqued my curiosity.'

The interpreter walked over to his desk.

'I'm glad to be of assistance. Anything you wish.'

He put the paper in his pocket and left the room.

When the examining magistrate got out of bed the next morning he noted that his cat, asleep on its pillow next to the bed, had deteriorated further. He left instructions regarding medication with his servant and left for the office with a heavy heart certainly, but not without a sense of eager anticipation. He had two very interesting appointments that morning: the monk who had followed the others like a shadow to the baron's estate, and the head of this strange party, the famous bee-keeper himself.

When he arrived, he found Paschalis waiting outside, and a rather elderly interpreter, apparently the only one available at such short notice, already in position. He was a little hard of hearing but otherwise of completely sound mind.

'Where were you last Friday at daybreak?'

'In my room. Not in the main building; in the servants' quarters.'

'Were you awake?'

'Yes, I was. I was praying.'

'Was it quiet?'

'Hardly. The birds on the lake were making a lot of noise, as usual, but I didn't think anything of it.'

'When were you informed of the baron's death?'

'I heard the interpreter shouting. I couldn't understand what he was saying, but I could hear him calling Mr Rosenmann. I went outside. He was very upset and told me he had found the baron drowned. Then everybody congregated down at the lake looking at the body.'

'Was the lake visible from your bedroom window?'

'A small section of it, yes.'

'Did you happen to look out in that direction before you heard the interpreter shouting?'

Paschalis thought for a moment.

'No, I don't think I did. If I did, I didn't notice anything unusual.'

'Had you observed anything during the previous days which made you think that the baron had made any enemies? Any incidents? Any conversations?'

Paschalis paused.

'I don't know.'

'You don't know what?' asked the examining magistrate, suspecting that the witness in black had something on his mind.

'I don't know if…I can…the truth is there was someone who had perhaps started to take a disliking to him, quite a strong one, in fact. But I'm not saying that this person killed him.'

'Which person?'

'I really don't want to cast suspicion for no good reason.'

'You have an obligation to testify to everything you know. If the individual concerned is innocent, they have nothing to fear. Who is this person?'

'The baron's friend, Mr Rosenmann.'

The examining magistrate looked at him in astonishment.

'Well?'

'I had noticed that Mr Rosenmann looked very disgruntled each time he saw the baron alone in conversation with Rodakis. Perhaps he was worried that…'

Paschalis broke off mid-sentence.

'Go on,' said the examining magistrate.

'Do you know why we were all there?'

'I am aware of the plans regarding honey production. I am also aware of the bee-keeper's amnesia.'

'Perhaps that was what Mr Rosenmann was afraid of, that Rodakis had remembered the formula and was renegotiating with the baron behind his back. I'm quite sure that if Mr Rosenmann believed that treachery of that sort was taking place, he would hate the baron for it. The only thing I know is that he suspected something. As for the other matter...'

The examining magistrate wrote down the name Rosenmann, with two crosses next to it. Then he said:

'That would have been possible if the bee-keeper had recalled the secret formula...'

'I believe he had. Rodakis has remembered it but is looking out for his interests, as usual. And that's why Rosenmann might have thought that with the baron out of the picture, who had probably been offering more – '

'I see. I understand what you are thinking. What makes you so confident that the man had remembered the formula?'

'I've learned how to read his eyes; I've known him for many years.'

'Tell me – is the honey really everything it's cracked up to be?'

Paschalis smiled.

'Yes, it is.'

The examining magistrate wondered if he'd ever live to sample a drop of that precious distillation. Confident that the man sitting across from him would not be able to answer that question, he sent him away. His instincts told him that the reliability of that particular witness was probably limited.

One of the functionaries informed him that Rodakis had arrived and was instructed to show him in after five minutes. The magistrate needed time to organise his thoughts. How strange! The bee-keeper case looked like it was going to take him way beyond the investigation into the mysterious drowning.

When the five minutes were up, Rodakis appeared in front of him. The examining magistrate looked at him and suddenly had the feeling that he was looking at a painted representation of a human being that had detached itself from its canvas and had somehow acquired flesh and bones.

'Take a seat, Sir. Now, can you account for your whereabouts last Friday at daybreak?'

'I was in my room.'

'Were you awake?'

'I had been asleep, but was woken by the shouts of the staff. The baron had just been found. I joined everybody else down at the lake. I saw the drowned baron too.'

'Before you were woken by the voices, had you been disturbed at all?'

'Nothing.'

'The night before? Anything unusual take place?'

'No. No. Nothing out of the ordinary.'

'Do you think it was an accident?'

'It's not impossible. The baron was an early riser. He frequently went down to the lake and fed the geese himself. He could have slipped.'

'Indeed. Anyway, who would want to push him in the water? The baron didn't have enemies.'

Rodakis continued to look at him with a face devoid of expression.

'Isn't that so?' The examining magistrate tried again.

'How would I be in a position to know that?'

'Judging from what you saw during your stay at his estate?'

'I wasn't there very long.'

'Everybody comments on how well-liked he was.'

'Yes, I think he was.'

'Did you pick up on any tension between the baron and his friend Mr Rosenmann?'

'None.'

'Were they close friends?'

'Very.'

'So there was nobody there who would want to harm the baron. Is that a fair assessment?'

'No Sir, I fear it isn't. There was someone who had recently become disenchanted with the baron.'

'Who?'

'A servant. Many years of service at the estate.'

'Tell me about him.'

'A few days before the accident, I was sitting in the dining room, quite innocently reading my book and the idiot managed to empty the contents of an entire bottle of red wine all over me. Naturally, I didn't mind about getting wet; I'm tougher than that, and besides, wine is a blessing. The problem was that the fool destroyed my book. It was an antiquarian book; one of a kind, utterly irreplaceable. I lost my composure, I must confess; I am very particular about my possessions. I lost control and the baron, listening to my shouts, became terribly distressed. The servant was fired on the spot; the baron gave him a week to leave the estate. The man started weeping but the baron was quite unmoved. Had it been over absolutely anything else, I would have intervened. But this was something I would never recover from and was not in a mood to be magnanimous over the incident. That was on the Saturday; he had to be out in a week. The baron was found dead on the Friday.'

'So you think that this servant would have gone as far as murdering the man he'd been so close to all those years?'

'I don't know. You'd better ask him that.'

The magistrate asked for the name of the servant, wrote it down, and drew three crosses next to it. Then, looking hard at Rodakis, asked:

'Any progress with your problem?'

'What problem?'

'I have been informed of the crisis you suffered with your memory concerning that short poem which holds the key to your formula. That problem.'

'What do you want me to tell you?'

'Are you still "in darkness"?'

'How is this relevant to the baron's drowning?'

'In a murder investigation, everything is relevant. You seem to forget that it is precisely because of your amnesia that you were guests of the baron at all. Please answer the question.'

'If I can remember the...?'

'Yes – if you can recall that short poem.'

'No,' answered Rodakis curtly.

After a short hesitation, the examining magistrate enquired:

'Is that an honest answer?'

'Yes,' confirmed Rodakis, in exactly the same tone.

'Do you think that it will ever come back to you?'

'The professor, Mr Rosenmann believes it will.'

'How did you come to make this discovery?' asked the examining magistrate with ardour. 'You are obliged to answer.'

'It was the result of prolonged research,' came the unruffled answer.

'Quite. But how did the idea occur to you in the first place? What led you to experiment in this way? Where did you get the idea from?'

'It came of its own accord.'

'Was it a difficult process, trying to arrive at the ideal combination?'

'Certainly wasn't simple.'

'Tell me about it.'

'It was difficult.'

'In what sense was it "difficult"?'

'In the sense that it wasn't easy.'

The examining magistrate paused. He realised that the more he insisted, the less progress he would make. He had begun to wonder whether Rodakis was deliberately mocking him, and accordingly shifted his voice into its most serious tone.

'Your arrangement with Mr Rosenmann; tell me, what were the terms?'

'If I remember rightly, Mr Rosenmann was to be responsible for distribution and sales. That would be such a weight off my mind, and I could then concentrate the supervision of the hives

– and I would not have to reveal the formula.'

'If and when you ever recall the formula, I would strongly advise you, before you do anything else, to write it down somewhere. What did Mr Rosenmann stand to gain form this arrangement?'

'A proportion of the profits. We hadn't quite settled the amount.'

'If I understand correctly, the monk is also entitled to a small share.'

'A negligible amount.'

'And where are your hives to be kept?'

'Back home, of course. Most probably on my native island.'

'I wish you every success.'

'Thank you.'

'Who knows, I might pay you a visit one day.'

Rodakis shrugged his shoulders in indifference at the prospect.

'That will be all for the moment. You might be required to come back, however,' he added, coldly, signalling to Rodakis that he could leave. Shortly thereafter, he dismissed the ancient interpreter too, and told him to report the following morning. Concerned that his words had fallen on deaf ears, he repeated the precise time twice.

The first thing the examining magistrate saw when he woke up the following morning was his cat, dead on its pillow. He picked up the pillow, the cat still lying on it, and lifted it onto the bed. Before leaving for the office, he left strict instructions not to allow anyone to enter the bedroom.

Rosa was ten minutes late. The examining magistrate instructed her to speak up when she gave her answers and began his interrogation.

'Can you account for your whereabouts last Friday at daybreak when the baron's body was found? Where you in your room?'

'Yes. I was asleep.'

'Were you woken by shouts?'

'No. I didn't hear a thing. My father came and woke me, but that was much later. He didn't say anything about the baron to begin with; didn't want to upset me, I suppose. I didn't find out until the afternoon and he wouldn't let me go to the room where the baron had been laid out to pay my respects because the stomach was all bloated and he was worried that the sight of it would scare me.'

'Was he right to worry?'

'I was upset even without seeing him. He was a really nice person.'

'Was everybody else just as upset as you were?'

'Yes, everybody was.'

'Mr Rosenmann? The servants?'

'Yes. Everybody. Some of them were even crying.'

'Even the manservant who had lost his job after spilling wine all over your father and ruining his book?'

'I don't know. Everybody was upset.'

'Was the baron an early riser?'

'I really don't know.'

'What about the servants? The cook, the gardeners, were they all up early? Did you hear them in the mornings – noises or talking?'

'I'm a really heavy sleeper, and my bedroom – the yellow one – was at the end of the corridor so I never heard anything, ever. My father never unlocked my door (I always go to sleep with my door locked) very early anyway. But that day, yes. Everybody was up; but I can't say how long they'd been up.'

'I take it you are no longer staying at the mansion.'

'No, I'm not. We moved to a hotel the same day. It's not as nice as at the baron's but we won't be there forever. At least I had time to say goodbye to the geese; I think they liked me. I don't care if they were squawky; they were nice. Anyway, it's not as if people don't make any noise, is it?'

'You're absolutely right,' said the examining magistrate, fending off the image of his dead cat stretched out on its pillow at the same time.

'I imagine that you, along with everybody else, are impatient for your father to recall his formula.'

'Oh no. Not at all, Sir!' Rosa's voice was raised. 'I'm praying that he never remembers it, never, never.'

The examining magistrate looked at her in bewilderment.

'Sir – my father has been found – alive. That's all the happiness I need. I had been without him for such a long time, all because of that formula. I'm sure that if he remembers it, it will only bring us more misery. From the moment he found it, terrible things started happening. First I lost my mother. She left the house one day (something she never did) and never came back. Struck by lightning. And then they got my father. Why? Because they wanted him to share his formula, his secret. And all those people coming up to the house, day in and day out, begging for honey, never leaving us alone. Please let him never remember. Please!'

'Surely other things happened too? Good things. You got to stay in a mansion and play with geese…'

'I suppose so. But the baron's dead, isn't he? No good will ever come of it, believe me. Best left alone.'

'Don't you think it would be an awful waste if such a remarkable discovery is lost?'

'Nothing gets lost. Everything is recorded in special ledgers.'

'I don't follow.'

Rosa took a deep breath and launched into her explanation:

'When I was little, my father used to tell me all about the ledgers with the secrets. All the big secrets in the world are recorded in them. There's not a secret on this Earth that can't be found in one of them, as long as there is no way that it could be discovered here. So, if my father never remembers the formula, or the poem for the formula, it will be saved in the pages of one of the ledgers.'

'I see,' said the examining magistrate, shooting a glance at the old interpreter who was obviously enjoying himself immensely.

'It might sound silly to you, but I still believe that those ledgers exist and are out there somewhere in space.'

'One thing's for sure: nobody can prove that they don't exist.'

'I always say to my father: imagine how good it will feel when you're dead, leafing through all those ledgers, and you come across the verse that unlocks the secret formula, and you'll say: "Fancy that! Such a simple little verse and I couldn't remember it!" '

The magistrate smiled a wan, uncomfortable smile.

'There are things I'd like to find out too,' Rosa went on. 'I'd try to find out, for example, why my mother suddenly went off like that the day the lightning hit her, where she went, what she wanted to do. I'd really like to know.'

The examining magistrate lowered his gaze and thought that he wouldn't mind knowing what had been going through his cat's head every time it had looked its owner in the eye.

'When I was really little, I couldn't wait to die so I could get to the ledgers. Now that I've grown up, I'm not in such a hurry to read them. I'll see them eventually.'

The magistrate turned to the interpreter, and said: 'Well, it certainly makes the thought of death somehow easier to live with, doesn't it?'

Returning to Rosa: 'Do you believe that the baron's death was an accident?'

'Very unlucky, yes.'

'You don't think that somebody wished him harm?'

'I don't know. There's a lot of wickedness in the world. But in the baron's case, I doubt it. Everybody liked him.'

The interrogation seemed to be drawing to a close.

'I enjoyed our little chat. And don't worry yourself – all of you will be free to go soon enough. I wish you the very best and hope everything turns out the way you hope it will. Run along now – your father is waiting for you outside. And we still have a number of statements to go through in order to throw some light on the case.'

Rosa stood up and was about to leave when all of a sudden she started laughing. She couldn't help herself – it was as though she had realised that what she was intending to say would sound ridiculous.

'Why throw light on the case? Why don't you just leave it in the dark? When the time comes and we're all dead, we can just consult the ledgers, and then we'll find out everything we need to know about the baron's death...'

The two men looked at each other. Gravely at first. But as the girl's uninhibited laughter intensified, the first twitches of a smile started to break through, almost instantly exploding into equally unchecked peals of laughter, laughter which could be heard all over the building.

stoLen time
by Vangelis Hatziyannidis

★ From the author of *Four Walls* ★

The second novel from Vangelis Hatziyannidis again stems
from the author's fascination with the way people act
when confined or imprisoned in some way.

A young and poverty-stricken student agrees to spend two
weeks in a remote hotel with a group of strangers for
the equivalent of five month's rent. He is interviewed about
his beliefs and his past by members of the group, who
occasionally mock him but never resort to violence.

The discovery of a list of names and dates written on a
wardrobe drawer in his room makes the young man curious
about previous 'guests' of the group. His unease increases when he
finds a concealed room and its alarming contents.

It is only years later that he is able to look back on what
took place in the hotel and begin to piece all the
parts of the puzzle together...

Translated from the Greek by Anne-Marie Stanton-Ife

ISBN: 0-7145-3126-X • SPRING 2007 • £9.99/$14.95

The Flea Palace

by Elif Shafak

★ Shortlisted for the *Independent* Prize for Foreign Fiction 2005 ★

The setting is a stately residence in Istanbul built by Russian noble émigré Pavel Antipov for his wife Agripina at the end of the Tsarist reign, now sadly dilapidated, flea-infested, and home to ten families. Shafak uses the narrative structure of *A Thousand and One Nights* to construct a story-within-a-story narrative.

Inhabitants include Ethel, a lapsed Jew in search of true love and the sad and beautiful Blue Mistress whose personal secret provides the novel with an unforgettable denouement. Add to this a strange, intensifying stench whose cause is revealed at the end of the book, and we have a metaphor for the cultural and spiritual decay in the heart of Istanbul.

'Once foundations are laid, this novel takes off into a hyper-active, hilarious trip, with farce, passion, mystery and many sidelights on Turkey's past. A cast of wacky flat-dwellers lend it punch and pizazz, from Ethel the ageing Jewish diva (a wonderful creation) to Gaba, the finest fictional dog in years.' *The Independent*

Translated from the Turkish by Müge Göçek

NEW £7.99 EDITION AVAILABLE NOW
ISBN: 0-7145-3120-0

The Gaze
by Elif Shafak

★ From the author of *The Flea Palace* ★

Shafak explores the subject of body image and desirability in women and men. An overweight woman and her lover, a dwarf, are sick of being stared at wherever they go, so decide to reverse roles. The man goes out wearing make up and the woman draws a moustache on her face.

The couple deal with the gaze of passersby in different ways. The woman wants to hide away from the world, while the man meets them head on, even compiling his own 'Dictionary of the Gaze' to show the powerful effects a simple look can have on a person's life.

The narrative of *The Gaze* is intertwined with the dwarf's dictionary entries and the story of a bizarre freak-show organized in Istanbul in the 1880s as the author explores the damage which can be done by our desire to look at other people.

Translated from the Turkish by Brendan Freely

ISBN: 0-7145-2121-9 • SUMMER 2006 • £9.99/$14.95

THE CIRCUMCISION
by György Dalos

A self-proclaimed 'Hungarian Communist Jew for Christ',
twelve-year-old Robi Singer has a lot on his plate. He is
a 'half-orphan', he is painfully overweight and what's
more, he has yet to be circumcised. With his Bar Mitzvah
fast approaching, the pressure is on. To make matters worse, Robi's
not sure he wants to be Jewish at all.

As his hypochondriac mother is more concerned
about her secret affair with 'Uncle' Moric, Robi's only ally
against the teachers at his Jewish school is
his eccentric, headstrong grandmother. It seems everyone has an
opinion on what he should do, but ultimately Robi
must make his own decision.

'Wisdom and humour against the shadows of existence:
Dalos, like Isaac B. Singer, is a follower of the great Yiddish
literary traditions.' *The Giessener Anzeiger*

Translated from the Hungarian by Judith Sollosy

ISBN: 0-7145-3123-5 • SPRING 2006 • £8.99/$14.95